*"I'll go with you. Who knows what
may lurk within the apartment
itself?"*

Greg took her arm to accompany her down the hall.

Jodie unlocked the door. The apartment was dark. "Anybody home?" she called. No answer. She felt for the light switch, and the apartment came into view. The empty room dispelled her fear and she said, "Now are you satisfied, or do you insist on looking under the bed, too?"

"Good idea!"

"Go home, Greg, and stop feeling you have to protect the whole world."

"Not the whole world. Just the people who matter to me," he said.

"Sorry," she said. "I didn't mean to snap. I guess it's nerves."

"That's all right. I want to see you in all your moods." Greg gazed at her, and a small _____ y smile curved his lips.

Jodie looked at him ___

"Jodie—" He pulle____
kissed her.

Dear Reader:

1990 is in full swing, and so is Silhouette Romances' tenth anniversary celebration—the DIAMOND JUBILEE! To symbolize the timelessness of love, as well as the modern gift of the tenth anniversary, we're presenting readers with a DIAMOND JUBILEE Silhouette Romance title each month, penned by one of your favorite Romance authors.

This month, visit the American West with Rita Rainville's *Never on Sundae*, a delightful tale sure to put a smile on your lips. Losing weight is never so romantic as when Wade Mackenzie is around. He has lovely Heather Brandon literally pining away! Then, in April, Peggy Webb has written a special treat for readers—*Harvey's Missing*. Be sure not to miss this heartwarming romp about a man, a woman and a lovable dog named Harvey!

Victoria Glenn, Annette Broadrick, Dixie Browning, Lucy Gordon, Phyllis Halldorson—to name just a few—have written DIAMOND JUBILEE titles especially for you.

And that's not all! This month we have a very special surprise! Ten years ago, Diana Palmer published her very first romance. Now, some of them are available again in a three-book collection entitled Diana Palmer Duets. Each book will have two wonderful stories plus an introduction by the author. Don't miss them!

The DIAMOND JUBILEE Celebration, plus special goodies like Diana Palmer Duets, is Silhouette Books' way of saying thanks to you, our readers. We've been together for ten years now, and with the support you've given to us, you can look forward to many more years of heartwarming, poignant love stories.

I hope you'll enjoy this book and all of the stories to come. Come home to romance—Silhouette Romance—for always!

Sincerely,

Tara Hughes Gavin
Senior Editor

JOAN SMITH

Sealed with a Kiss

Silhouette Romance

Published by Silhouette Books New York

America's Publisher of Contemporary Romance

SILHOUETTE BOOKS
300 E. 42nd St., New York, N.Y. 10017

ISBN: 0-373-08711-X

First Silhouette Books printing March 1990

Printed in the U.S.A.

Books by Joan Smith

Silhouette Romance

JOAN SMITH

has written many Regency romances but likes working with the greater freedom of contemporaries. She also enjoys mysteries and Gothics, collects Japanese porcelain and is a passionate gardener. A native of Canada, she is the mother of three.

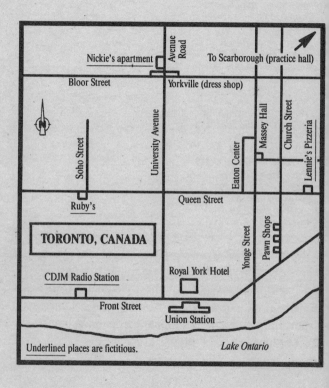

Chapter One

Hello, Mom. Have you heard from Hank?'' Jodie asked as soon as she got home. Tossing her shoulder bag over the back of a chair, she sat down, exhausted.

Her mother was sitting in the tidy little kitchen, staring at a cold cup of tea on the table and looking too tired to speak. Her usually cheerful face was drawn into worry lines, and her hair looked as if it hadn't been combed that day. "No," she said, shaking her head, "I didn't really expect to hear from him this soon. The local police have contacted the Toronto police, and they'll keep an eye out. I've been speaking to Gil's mother on the phone. She's very worried, too. He didn't even leave her a note."

"What a thoughtless jerk," Jodie said, and went to give her mother a reassuring hug. "At least Hank would never pull a stunt like that on us." Not that his brief note was much consolation:

Mom,
I have gone with SWAK to start our career. Don't worry about us. We'll be fine. I love you.

Hank

P.S. Take care of Duke.

Duke, Hank's beagle, was lying in front of the screen door to the backyard, mourning. He lifted his head from his paws and gave a pitiful whine.

"Bud Edison is the oldest boy," Mrs. James said. "He must be the one who put them up to it."

"There's no point playing the blame game, Mom," Jodie said, while pouring herself a glass of orange juice. Finding no sign of dinner, she lingered at the refrigerator, resting her back against the door, as she perused its contents.

Of course she didn't expect her mother to carry on as if nothing had happened, when her teenage son had just run off from home with his friends to become a rock star. They hadn't discovered Hank was gone till that morning. He often stayed out late practicing during the holidays, or playing in the local clubs with his group. Jodie had phoned her boss, asking for the day off to try to find Hank. It helped that her boss was Mr. Edison, older brother of Bud, who was the leader of the group. Mr. Edison was in complete agreement about getting the boys back as soon as possible, though she noticed he hadn't mentioned the day off himself.

She knew that his management consulting company was reaching the crucial stage of an important merger, and Mr. Edison was very busy, but she'd have thought his brother would be his first priority. Jodie had joined Edison's staff a year ago as a programmer for the newly formed computer consulting services division. She knew Mr. Edison to speak to, but didn't have much personal contact with him. He kept a polite social distance from his employees, especially ones on the junior level like her, who'd only been there a year.

"You didn't learn anything from Hank's friends?" her mother asked hopefully.

"No, nothing. I only managed to get in touch with a few of them. If they know anything, they aren't talking." It was the first week of the summer holidays. At least the runaways had passed their final exams before leaving.

"I imagine they went to Toronto, as you once did," Mrs. James said, with an admonishing look at Jodie.

This running away from home seemed to be a rite of passage in the James family. After seeing a production of *Swan Lake*, Jodie had wanted to become a ballet dancer. She hadn't waited till the end of the school year, but had gone to Toronto during the Easter holidays when she was sixteen to try out for the National Ballet Company. She had made the mistake of going to stay with relatives, which enabled her father to get her back within a week. She realized now that he'd known where she was from the first night, and had let her have her little adventure, to work it out of her system. Of course she had been hopelessly undertrained in ballet, and was ultimately not accepted.

The incident had brought her hopes of a dancing career to a halt, but it had convinced her dad that his dreams of his daughter's attending agricultural college and running the family farm were not to be realized. He allowed her to study computer science, which was her second career choice. When her father had died during her last year at the university, the farm was sold. What remained of the family moved the five miles to Waterloo, which was closer to the university. It was a small city, but cultured and close to Toronto.

"Hank's just turned seventeen," Mrs. James said uncertainly. "He's not old enough to be on his own. Oh, I do hope he returns to finish his last year of high school, in case the music doesn't work out. That way he'll be able to go on to study something else. He always talked about being a vet. You know how he loves animals." She glanced at Duke, who gave her a sad-eyed look of accusation. "If we'd stayed on the farm when your dad died, Hank never would have fallen in with that rock crowd."

Jodie knew the disparagement was meant for the music, not the boys involved. Mrs. James genuinely liked Bud and Gil. Casting recriminations was an exercise in futility. "How could we run the farm without Dad? It was already too much for him. Have you eaten anything?" Jodie asked, changing the subject.

Her mother just looked at her with melancholy eyes. "I forgot all about dinner. I keep picturing poor little Hank, alone in Toronto. You hear such stories about the city." She gave a shudder.

"He's not so little anymore, Mom. He's six feet tall," Jodie reminded her. "And he's with Gil and Bud. Nobody's going to attack three husky young men. It's not as if they're little kids. They don't do drugs or anything. They'll be all right, but I still plan to find them and bring Hank back. I'll give him a good piece of my mind for running off like that, too. It's so stupid!"

She stopped and frowned. Hank was only half a year older than she'd been when she made her foray into the ballet world. He wasn't really stupid, he was just young and inexperienced, perhaps looking for a little excitement. Personally, she blamed Bud Edison. He was the older one—a year older and the venerated leader of the group. Despite his obvious influence over the boys, he was a darned good musician. She had been glad when Bud asked Hank to join SWAK. Hank had been a new kid in school, without friends, and lonesome after his dad's death. The band had seemed to be a great outlet until now.

SWAK wasn't a tough heavy metal group, or a punk group. They played nice civilized jazz rock. High school dances were the source of their major engagements, or gigs, as they referred to them, and the group was popular. Bud was the composer, arranger, lead guitarist and prime mover in the whole band. He also played keyboards. Hank played bass; Gil Turner played drums. Of the three, Jodie thought Bud might actually become a professional musician one day. Of course the snooty Mr. Edison loathed the idea, although he'd paid for Bud's piano lessons since he was six. Mr. Edison's attitude was probably responsible for desperate measures.

It was no secret his brother wanted him to go to Harvard to study business, now that he'd finished high school. Bud used to talk about Juilliard. He'd secretly applied there and got accepted. He'd even gone to New York for the audition during the Easter holidays by pretending he was going to visit Harvard for a look-see. Mr. Edison hadn't had any objection to that, of course! He had arranged for Bud to help out at his office for the summer, to begin learning the ropes.

"He wants to make a bean counter out of me!" Bud had exclaimed indignantly. "An accountant, imagine!"

Jodie shook the wisp of memory away. "I'll make us some dinner," she said, returning to the refrigerator. Looking inside, she found a roast chicken, which she'd overlooked in her earlier search. Her mother had managed to prepare it some time during that hectic day. Jodie sliced it, put buns in the oven to warm and made a salad. It was a warm June day, and a cold dinner would be fine. She put Duke out, much to his dislike.

Her mother only pecked at her dinner. Jodie couldn't eat much, either. She tried to keep up a cheerful front for her mom's sake, but deep down, she was worried. She had to get Hank back and convince him to finish his final year of high school. He was just too young to start bashing his head against the iron door of the music world. He needed at least to acquire his high school diploma. She still hoped she could convince him to go to agricultural college after graduation. He had always loved the animals on the neighbors' farm. If her dad had had a dairy farm instead of growing crops, they probably would have kept the place.

"I'll tell you what I'll do, Mom," she said, after they had both given up the pretense of eating. "I'll take a few days off work and go down to Toronto. I'm sure Mr. Edison won't mind, especially since Bud's involved, too. I'll ask around and see if I can get a lead on the boys' whereabouts."

"We don't know that they went to Toronto."

"They couldn't go to the States without green cards. Toronto's the biggest city in the country, and also the closest. They've got to be there."

"You always were the logical one in the family," her mother said, nodding. "I guess that's why you're so good at computers."

Jodie didn't mention that looking for the boys would be like looking for a needle in a haystack. How many hundreds of young people ran off to the city every year? At least she had one contact who could help her. Her classmate, Nickie Sommers, worked for a rock radio station. She worked in the accounts department, but she could ask the disk jockeys if they'd heard of a new local group. Jodie had one other pale hope. Bud Edison had taken his dilapidated old van to carry their gear, and that might be spotted more easily than the boys.

"Shouldn't I go with you?" her mother asked.

Jodie bit back a smile. She could just see her mom, a respectable, middle-aged lady, dealing with the Queen Street

milieu. She didn't relish the thought herself. Aspiring artists and writers and musicians had claimed the quarter
around Queen Street for their own. The area was close to
downtown, slowly progressing toward gentrification.
Therefore, the rents were cheap, especially if divided three
ways. She was certain the boys would flock there as if by
instinct.

"You don't have to do that, Mom," she said. "Nickie will
help me. I've been there before with her. I won't be in any
danger, if that's what you're worried about."

"I'd probably just be in your way. I'll tell Gil's mother.
She'll be relieved to hear you're going." Mrs. Turner was a
widow, too, and Gil was her only child. There was no one
else to help her. "It's odd Mr. Edison hasn't done anything
about it," she added, picking up the phone.

Jodie had been pondering that, too. Mr. Edison was the
obvious one to take the lead. Apart from the fact that Bud
was the oldest and had almost certainly put the others up to
running away, the Edisons were a wealthy and influential
family. The great Gregory Edison could have pulled a few
strings with the police. Maybe he was just too disgusted with
a younger brother who refused to go to Harvard and add to
the family fortune. She knew Bud didn't get along with his
brother. He spent as much time as possible right here with
Hank, eating her mother's homemade cookies and drinking their milk.

"I'll call Mr. Edison about getting a few days off after
you talk to Mrs. Turner," she said.

Jodie cleared the table and stacked the dishwasher while
her mother used the phone. Then she went to the living
room and sat, mentally arranging her trip.

Hotels were expensive in the city. She'd see if Nickie could
put her up in Toronto. The thing to do would be to hang out
around Queen Street, and try to develop a quick friendship
with some of the musicians there. They wouldn't give a

straight businesswoman the time of day. She'd have to disguise herself as a teenage fan.

She'd wear jeans and T-shirts and leave her hair free and long, to appear younger. It was a good thing no one from the office would see her. She went to the opposite extreme at work, trying to appear more mature by wearing tailored clothes, pulling her long hair back in a neat bun. To cut down on computer glare, she'd bought a pair of glare-proof glasses with dark rims that made her look studious.

Just as her mother came into the living room, there was a knock on the front door. They exchanged a look of alarm. A caller at this time might be bringing news of Hank. "I'll get it," Jodie said, and ran to the door.

The man standing there looked so somber and serious in his suit and tie that for a moment she was afraid it was a police detective, who'd come to make some awful announcement. Once the man moved into the light, his face became recognizable. And now she was standing face-to-face with her boss.

"Oh, Mr. Edison. Come in," she said. Jodie felt disconcerted to be caught out of her office uniform. For running around town trying to get news from Hank's friends, she was wearing a simple cotton dress and flat-heeled sandals, with her hair pulled back in a ponytail.

At first glance, Mr. Edison wasn't sure it was Miss James. He could see a resemblance—a younger sister, perhaps. Yet the girl seemed to know him. "Miss James?" he said questioningly.

She blinked in surprise. Good Lord, he didn't recognize her. "Yes, please come in," she repeated.

"Any news?" he asked eagerly, following her inside.

"Not really. My mother and I have been discussing it."

Jodie certainly wasn't ashamed of her house, but she realized Mr. Edison wasn't used to a modest little bungalow. He followed her into the living room, which was decorated with the old-fashioned country furnishings from the farm. His manners were excellent. He said all the right things, as he greeted Mrs. James, expressing his sympathy, urging them not to be too worried. He assured them both that he was doing everything he could to find the boys. She was relieved to hear it. She might have known Mr. Edison wouldn't just sit twiddling his thumbs, when his brother was missing.

"I've been hounding the police all day," he said. "I've managed to persuade them to send a plainclothes officer to Toronto. I found a recent photograph of the three boys in Bud's room and had copies made to be dispersed to all neighboring communities."

Jodie was happy to see that her mother was reassured. She felt reassured herself, at first. There was something in Gregory Edison that inspired confidence. He was a tall man, well built with wide shoulders. He had that sort of rugged, dark-complexioned good looks that made a woman feel safe. His deep, authoritative voice helped. So did his firm, craggy jaw and sympathetic eyes, which were a very dark blue. His whole appearance, so well dressed and prosperous, inspired confidence.

But as Jodie looked past this outer shell, she began to realize that Mr. Edison was out of his depths in this unusual situation. She thought he'd be great at recovering money from a crooked investor, or pursuing a felonious politician. He talked about the law, and the legal steps that could be taken, but the boys weren't criminals. They had just run away from home.

"There are thousands of runaways in Toronto," Jodie said. "I'm afraid one policeman who isn't even from Toronto isn't going to be much help."

"I realize that. I've also hired a private detective," he told her. "He specializes in finding runaways. Youngsters are in great danger in the city." He mentioned the rate of crime, drugs, prostitution, even murder.

Mrs. James listened with rising alarm. Jodie was relieved when the phone rang, to get her mother out of the room. She didn't want to be rude to her boss, but she had to warn him to stop that line of talk.

"I don't think we should emphasize the danger, Mr. Edison." He gave her a sharp, surprised look. At work, no one answered Mr. Edison back. Embarrassment lent a brusque edge to her warning. "My mother's worried enough as it is."

"There's no point sticking our heads in the sand," he replied curtly. "The boys *are* in danger."

"No one's going to force those three big boys, who are practically men, to do anything they don't want to," she retorted. Her nerves were taut, and she had only a minute to convince him.

Mr. Edison had never paid any particular attention to Miss James before. He knew she was a good, competent employee. He saw her occasionally, sitting at her computer, fingers busily typing. He had the impression she wore glasses, but she wasn't wearing them tonight. Her blond hair wasn't as tidy as she usually wore it. He had always thought she was a prim, respectful sort of woman, and was surprised that she spoke so sharply to him.

After looking more closely, he realized she was younger than he'd thought. Her eyes were bright and intelligent. Greenish eyes, with flecks of gold. They were a little tilted at the outer edge, giving her a feline quality. It must have been the glasses that changed her looks. Although young, she was perfectly mature.

"There's some safety in numbers," he admitted. "I hope Bud has enough sense to stay out of the seedy districts of town."

"He may have the sense, but he won't have the money," she said bluntly. "They're not going to be checking in at the ritzy Park Plaza."

Mr. Edison wasn't accustomed to being corrected so frankly. He felt his hackles rise, accompanied by an urge to put his employee in her rightful place. "I realize that, but there are smaller hotels that give quite reasonable weekly rates."

Jodie shook her head ruefully. The man was completely out of it. He'd been too well off for too long to know how struggling kids survived. She had known plenty of poor students who were forced to work in order to support themselves through college. "Any kind of hotel is completely beyond their range. What they'll probably do is rent a bedroom each, or maybe share one or two. If they get lucky, they'll find an inexpensive apartment."

He frowned, wondering how she knew so much about it. Bud occasionally mentioned Hank's sister, but he never implied that she had anything to do with the musical crowd. "Did your brother discuss this scheme with you?" he asked.

"No. I would have put a stop to it if he had," she said crossly. Her little pointed chin rose aggressively. This was a side of Miss James he would never have suspected existed. "I'd like to go to Toronto tomorrow to look for them, if you think the office can spare me," she said.

"Alone?" he asked, startled.

Jodie had to bite back her smile. You'd think she was walking into the jaws of death. "Alone," she replied.

"That's not a good idea, Miss James. If you're planning to look in the kinds of places we've been talking about, you might be in some danger yourself."

"Queen Street's not so dangerous. There's no point looking at the Park Plaza," she pointed out reasonably.

"Someone should go with you. If I didn't have the McMurchy merger coming up..."

Jodie tried not to sneer. She certainly didn't want to be burdened with Mr. Edison, but she wanted to let him know what she thought of him, putting money before his brother. "I realize how important that McMurchy case is to you," she said stiffly.

A blaze flared in his eyes. It was guilt, he knew, that caused that unreasonable anger, but dammit, it wasn't his fault! Why did he work so hard, if not to give Bud a better life than he'd had himself? "It's not more important than my brother! I've done everything possible to help Bud. I feel a little responsible since I'm the one who suggested music lessons in the first place, never dreaming he'd become a fanatic. I've told him dozens of times that this rock music is nonsense. He used to play Chopin beautifully, imagine!" He shook his head, sighing in regret. "Then he started playing a little electronic machine."

"It's called a Moog. Bud plays keyboards in the band, as well as lead guitar." And his own brother didn't even know it! He didn't seem very interested, either.

"It was all right for a hobby when he was in high school. It kept him out of worse trouble, but it's not a terribly reliable career. A hundred—a thousand—groups end up on skid row for everyone that makes it. And even if by some miracle he became successful, the career would be short-lived. He could end up on drugs...."

Jodie agreed with part of what he'd said. She, too, had hoped Hank's music would die a natural death when he finished high school, but to leap to the conclusion that all musicians turned to drugs was ludicrous. "I think you're overestimating the danger," she said.

"It's always wise to err on the down side. That way, you take the necessary precautions." This philosophy had served him well in business. He didn't see that the present case was any different in that respect.

"Very likely, but I hope you won't scare my poor mother to death. What precautions do you think are feasible?"

"I obviously have to get Bud back, before he falls into the hands of—"

Mrs. James came back before he could say more, but of course Jodie knew what he meant—before he fell into the hands of drug dealers.

"That was Mrs. Turner again," Mrs. James said. "She found Gil's bank book in his room. He's withdrawn his money from the bank. Three hundred dollars. Hank did the same. He had earned six hundred—from the concerts they've played. I expect Bud had something, too, Mr. Edison," she added, looking with interest to learn how much cash the boys had between them, to stave off starvation.

"The money I've set aside for Bud's education is tied up in a trust fund. He probably had a few hundred in his checking account," he replied.

"That's something," Mrs. James said.

"They'd have more than a thousand between them," he continued. "Still, they'd have to pay the first and last month's rent to get an apartment. That'd leave them flat broke." Mrs. James gave a wince of fear at his thoughtless speech.

Jodie felt a pronounced urge to throttle her boss, but limited her censure to a meaningful glare. "If they just took rooms, they'd probably pay by the week. And anyway, they'll get jobs to tide them over. All the musicians do that."

"What job can they possibly do?" he demanded, in a rhetorical spirit.

"Any number of things," Jodie said through gritted teeth. "They could pump gas, drive a delivery truck, work in a store or restaurant like the students I went to university with. Good tips in restaurants."

"An Edison slinging hash!" he growled, and frowned at the wall. Was this why he had knocked himself out, he thought, working to make a decent life for Bud? When their parents died, the judge had suggested Bud be put in a foster home. A college student couldn't take proper care of a younger brother, he had said. Well, he had proved the judge wrong. By working very hard, he had managed to clothe and feed Bud, and still finish his last year of college. There hadn't been much of an opportunity to establish a relationship with his kid brother. Between working and studying and keeping up the apartment, he hardly had time to do more than glance at Bud, to see whether his clothes were clean, and his hair combed. It had meant a lot of scrimping—subsisting on hamburger and pasta dinners, living in a little apartment, but once he graduated, that form of existence came abruptly to an end.

He had determined that he'd make up those first rough years to Bud, and he had done it. They lived the good life now, in a fine home. And he meant to see that Bud received a good education, so he'd never have to be poor again. "I'll lock him in his room when I get him home, then personally escort him to Harvard in the autumn," he said grimly.

"I expect that attitude's half the trouble," Jodie said, all at once amazed at her daring. But Mr. Edison was much too domineering. He seemed to take on the appearance of an ogre when he spoke about Harvard. This wasn't work, and he wasn't her boss in this house. She'd speak her mind. "Bud's eighteen, Mr. Edison. You can't keep an eighteen-year-old locked in his room."

"I obviously didn't mean that literally," he snapped.

Mrs. James knew her daughter was short-tempered, and jumped in to avoid offending their guest. "Would you like some tea, Mr. Edison?"

"No, thank you. I must be getting home. I have some work to do."

"It's very upsetting," Mrs. James said, shaking her head. "Oh well, they're not the first youngsters to have run off."

Jodie thought her mother would continue to tell of her daughter's youthful dreams of becoming a ballet dancer. She wasn't eager for Mr. Edison to hear that story. "We'll get them back," she said swiftly, to change the subject.

"I still don't think you should go to Toronto alone," Mr. Edison repeated. A young woman like Miss James might not be completely aware of the dangers awaiting her in a big city. Yet he wasn't one bit eager to go with her. The McMurchy deal was reaching the climax. He'd been working on it for two months. But more important, traveling with an employee—one who looked like Miss James—could become awkward. Besides, he hadn't much idea where to look.

Jodie lifted her green eyes to his and said, "My brother means a lot to me. I can't just sit here wringing my hands with worry."

He read a challenge in her speech. Her brother meant a lot to her implied that Bud didn't mean that much to him. He had lived for Bud. How dared she—His jaws clenched. He could let his partner finalize the McMurchy deal. The real work had already been done. "I'll go with you," he said.

"What a good idea!" Mrs. James beamed, with obvious relief. She had been taken in by his take-charge attitude; if Mr. Edison was on the job, it was as good as done. "I'll tell Mrs. Turner. I told her you were here, Mr. Edison. She was sure you'd find the boys." She fluttered off to the phone again, leaving Jodie alone with him.

"You don't have to come," Jodie said. She had got him to offer, though, and that was a minor success.

"My decision is made," he said gruffly. "I'll make the hotel arrangements tonight, and we'll leave early in the morning—seven or seven-thirty. It's a longish drive, but not long enough to bother with airports. We might as well travel together. I usually stay at the Plaza." He looked to see if this met with her approval.

She had a feeling he'd be like that, orchestrating the trip from A to Z. A needle of resentment pricked her, and she was happy to be able to deflate him. "I'll be staying with a friend, and we should either leave at six, or around nine. We don't want to hit the commuter rush to the city, or else we'd sit in traffic for hours."

He was annoyed that he hadn't thought of that himself. He was the boss, he should be the knowledgeable, in-charge one. But although he'd tried to remain in control, he was racked with worry at Bud's defection, and not thinking quite straight. "Yes, well, the sooner we get on with it, the better. I'll just reserve the one room then. We'll leave at six, if that's all right with you?"

"Fine, but you really don't have to come, Mr. Edison."

"My brother's got involved somehow in this ridiculous scheme. I'll go."

He said it as though Hank and Gil had talked his brother into their escapade. He also sounded as though he were being noble, when he was just doing his duty. Jodie felt an uncontrollable spurt of anger and spoke sharply. "Your brother was the instigator of the whole plan, if you ask me. He's the oldest one, and the leader of the band. Maybe you should go."

She received an angry glare from his navy-blue eyes. "He may be the leader of the band, but I think he had a little encouragement from his friends," he retorted. His accusing look seemed to concentrate on Jodie.

"We all encouraged the boys musically, although I certainly didn't have anything to do with this caper, if that's what you're thinking. What they should have done was get organized, make a plan, lease an apartment and let us know they were going."

He looked at her as though she'd suggested robbing a bank. "What they should have done was forget the whole thing, and apply themselves to their studies. Bud has a first-rate brain, if he'd only use it. I don't know what the other boys might have planned for their future, but Bud has a good job waiting for him. He nearly didn't make it into Harvard, with this rock and roll foolishness. I had to twist a few arms."

"Including Bud's!" she flashed out. His egotism was enough to madden a saint. "Maybe he doesn't want to be a business tycoon."

Who wouldn't want to be a successful businessman? The idea was nonsense. "He's still young and immature. He'll thank me when he's older."

"Will he?" Jodie asked, and just looked at him, with those tilted cat eyes. She didn't expect an answer, but she hoped he'd think about it. It was no mean feat to get accepted at the prestigious Juilliard School of Music. If Mr. Edison had let Bud go to Juilliard as he wanted to, this would never have happened.

He ignored her question. "Since we're leaving early, I'd better go home and pack. You'll be ready at six?"

"Ready and waiting. I suggest you wear comfortable shoes. We'll be pounding a lot of pavement."

When he left, Jodie sat on, thinking. Mr. Edison would be more of a nuisance than anything else. She'd let him work with the private detective he'd hired, while she got the inside dope from Nickie, and followed that course. It would give her some satisfaction to be the one who succeeded. Her boss needed to be taught a lesson. He took himself much too seriously, and the rest of the world not seriously enough.

When her mother finally got off the phone, Jodie called her friend Nickie Sommers in Toronto, and arranged to stay with her. The great Mr. Edison would be staying at the Park Plaza in the chic Bloor Street district, which was fine. The farther away from her, the better. She didn't want to come to blows and lose her job, but if she had to listen to much more of his arrogant nonsense she wouldn't be able to control herself.

After she told Nickie her problem, she went to her room to decide what clothes to take. She had dreaded having to appear in front of Mr. Edison dressed as a teenager, but now the idea was beginning to amuse her. She racked her brain to come up with an idea that would give her an *in* with the rock crowd.

To talk to the local groups without inciting too much curiosity, she'd pose as someone trying to join a rock band. Since she couldn't play any instruments, she'd have to pretend she was a singer. She had been in the glee club at school, and still sang in the shower for her own enjoyment. She might manage to pass herself off as a singer in a fledgling band.

She packed her jeans and some summer tops. Sneakers were necessary for pavement pounding. Since she didn't like to wear sneakers without socks, she threw in some white athletic socks. Once he saw her in this sort of attire, Mr. Edison would probably refuse to let her in his car tomorrow.

When her bag was packed, she pulled the clasp off her hair to brush it out before going to bed. Her hair was naturally blond, but she highlighted the front of it. It looked best brushed out loose around her face, but she only wore it that way for dates. Tomorrow, she'd wear it that way, since it made her look younger.

She braided it before going to bed. The contours of her face were revealed, making her look more mature and dignified. More like the boring kind of woman Mr. Edison was probably prone to go out with, she thought. He hadn't asked her to call him Gregory, she noticed. She didn't intend to let him stand up on his pedestal, looking down at her. He'd likely wear his two-piece suit, and a shirt and tie, scaring off anybody he talked to.

On this thought, she turned out the light and went to bed. Tomorrow was going to be a busy day.

Chapter Two

Gregory Edison literally didn't recognize Jodie James when he saw her standing on the curb waiting for him the next morning. From half a block away, he saw the girl in jeans with one foot on the curb, one on the road, looking for oncoming cars. Because she carried two large bags, one of which was slung over her shoulder, he thought she might be a teenage hitchhiker. He was almost sorry that he had to pull close to the curb beside her. She'd probably try to jump into his car. He checked to make sure the door on the far side was locked.

He noticed she was dressed casually in jeans, a loose shirt, socks and sneakers. As he drew closer, he saw her hair, which was blond as Miss James's was, but worn hanging loose behind, with a kerchief to keep it out of her eyes. Nice hair, he thought, if only the girl knew what to do with it. Those jeans didn't leave much to the imagination. The way kids dressed today!

He didn't see her face until he has stopped in front of the Jameses' house, and he still didn't recognize her.

The girl ran to his car as soon as he stopped, as he was afraid she would. He rolled down his window and said, "I'm sorry, miss. I wasn't stopping to give you a lift. I have to pick—" He stopped in midspeech. He recognized those gold-flecked, green eyes. But what accounted for the smile? It was a grin really, laughing at his mistake.

"Don't worry, Mr. Edison. It's only me," she replied. He felt like an idiot. He reached over and unlocked the door, and she hopped in. She tossed one bag in the back seat and put her big shoulder bag at her feet. Where was her luggage? Good Lord, was that all she'd packed?

"I'm afraid I didn't recognize you in that—er, outfit," he said. Was it possible Miss James always dressed in this manner away from the office? He didn't want to offend her, but really! Surely for a trip to the city with her boss, she might have worn a dress.

Jodie felt a little spurt of something at his reaction, although she couldn't define whether it was amusement or annoyance. He'd been in an ivory tower too long. This brush with reality might be just what Mr. Edison needed to jolt him out of his arrogance. "I dressed to blend in with the surroundings of where we're going. This is nothing compared to what you'll see before the day's over," she replied blandly. No apologies, no embarrassment. He was the one who'd look out of place before long.

He turned a dark blue eye on her and said blandly, "You don't have to apologize, Miss James. What you wear away from the office is your own business. I realize that my younger employees find my office dress code a little strict, but I deal with important clients, and they expect business people to look the part."

So that was what he thought of her, that she'd be wearing this to the city without a good reason! She didn't much care for that inference of belonging to the "younger" category, either, but she let it pass. "Let's step on the gas and beat the rush," she suggested, as if she were talking to one of her friends.

Mr. Edison turned on the ignition and the motor hummed softly. Jodie reached into her purse, which was as big as a suitcase, and took out a pair of dark glasses. They were large and round, with pink rims. She slid them on and said, "I hope you brought your shades. We'll be driving into the sun."

"I keep a pair in the glove compartment."

She reached for it as he took off. It was locked. "You're the careful type, huh?" she said, and laughed.

She had a nice laugh, deep and natural, but Mr. Edison was struck with the idea that she was laughing at him. She thought he was an old fogy. "Why make it easy for a car thief to get his hands on my ownership papers?" he asked reasonably.

"I guess you have to be careful with expensive wheels like this. What is it? A Jaguar?" She looked around at the expensive leather interior and the complicated dashboard.

"Yes," he said briefly.

He wasn't one to brag about his material possessions, but she figured he probably liked the best of everything. He certainly wore beautiful suits to work, and she knew his house in old Westmount was an impressive half-timber and brick building that looked as if it belonged in the English countryside.

While he drove, she took a moment to survey his mode of dress for this occasion. He looked less formally attired than last night, but much dressier than Jodie felt necessary. He wore a striped sport shirt, open at the neck, and light trousers. A quick glance showed her he had taken her advice and wore what he probably considered to be casual shoes. Polished Italian loafers, however, were only casual in comparison with what he usually wore.

"Sorry about, uh, not recognizing you back there, Miss James," he said. It seemed absurd, calling this ragamuffin Miss James. The jeans, he noticed, were well-worn, and so were the sneakers.

"I told you, I dressed for the occasion," she said offhandedly. Were they going to go on calling each other "Miss James" and "Mr. Edison" throughout their trip? She was a little disappointed that he didn't say anything more about her outfit. She had looked forward to shocking him, but the quivering of his lips told her he was only amused. Was he laughing at her? "When in Rome, you know," she added.

"Of course." Definitely he was laughing, and trying not to show it.

"Well, we aren't going to look for the boys in boardrooms, are we? They'll be on the streets." She ignored his quivering lips and said, "We were lucky to get such nice weather for the trip. I have some fruit in my purse, in case you haven't had breakfast."

"I've had breakfast, but you go ahead."

Jodie took out an orange and peeled it, wrapping the rinds up in a napkin and putting them back in her purse. She ate silently till they reached the highway. She was a little miffed with Gregory Edison. "You should stop and get those sunglasses out of the glove compartment before we hit the highway."

"A good idea." He pulled in and did as she suggested. He had been doing some thinking, and had come to the conclusion that Hank's sister would have a better chance of finding the boys than a detective, or himself. She apparently visited Toronto often and had close friends there. She was younger than he, too, and she had kept in closer touch with her brother. As a managing consultant, Greg realized that she was his most valuable tool, and since he had to work with her, he wanted to keep the relationship friendly.

"I'd like to make my base of operations as handy as possible to the area where the boys would be hanging out," he said. "That'd be the bohemian part of town. The Queen Street area, isn't it?"

"Yes, that area." She had hoped to have to tell him these things, and was annoyed that he knew about Queen Street. The only thing she could take exception to was his use of the old-fashioned word *bohemian*. "You didn't make a reservation at the Plaza then?"

"I hoped you could suggest something more convenient."

"You wouldn't be happy at any of the really convenient places, but old downtown's handier than Yorkville."

"Maybe you're right. I'll want a shower and a good bed after a hard day's looking, preferably without hot and cold running cockroaches. The Royal York will do. Where does your—friend live?"

Now why did he hesitate over the word *friend*? Did he think she was staying with a man? "Nickie lives quite far away, on Avenue Road, north of Bloor." She smiled to herself. The name wouldn't tell him much. Nickie could be either a man or a woman.

"What time do you want to go there?" he asked.

"Not until tonight. I only plan to sleep there. I'll check my bag at Union Station and pick it up tonight. The subway goes there, no problem."

"You might as well leave it in my room. The Royal York's practically next door."

And she'd have to go to his room to pick it up.... Was that why he was wondering whether Nickie was a man? Was it possible Mr. Edison planned to misbehave, away from the prying eyes of home? No, it was beyond the realm of possibility that he had any designs on her virtue. He was trying to be helpful, so she decided to go along with him. "It'll save a quarter," she said.

His next speech was as good as an announcement that he was going out of his way to be agreeable. "If you want to listen to some rock, feel free. You might enjoy some music while we ride."

So he'd concluded she was a rocker, had he? She already knew his opinion of rock music, and it stood to reason that he'd hold a biased view of people who listened to it. "Thanks, but I concentrate better without it."

"Are you working out a plan?" he asked hopefully.

"Frankly, I have very little idea where to begin. What do you think the boys would have done, when they reached Toronto?"

"First, find digs—I mean, find a place to stay. Secondly, probably find a job."

"There must be hundreds of little bars that hire bands. This could take weeks."

Obviously Bud Edison had never dared discuss his plans within earshot of Mr. Edison. She had been listening to the boys talk for months, but had always thought it was dream talk. When she was that age, she and her friends used to discuss becoming models, but deep in their hearts, they knew it wouldn't happen.

"Hank said the bars don't hire unknown bands," she explained. "They book through managers. At home, the group played the high school circuit mostly. Since the schools are closed for the summer, they won't pick up any gigs there—I mean the kinds of jobs we talked about last night."

Greg bit back the phrase *slinging hash*. He'd done plenty of that demeaning work himself. It hurt to think of Bud sinking so low. "The employment agencies might give us a line on them," he mentioned.

"My friends at university never bothered with agencies. They're too slow. There are all sorts of clerk and food service jobs that you can get without an agency's help. Maybe they'll wait a day or two before they even try. They'll be eager to try to meet some other groups, to learn the ropes. One of the first things they'll do is make a demo tape. They didn't have one, and Bud said no manager would even look at them till they had something on tape for him to hear."

Bud said.... She spoke of him so casually, as if they were friends. Why hadn't Bud said any of this to him? He could have talked his brother out of this folly if he'd only known of it. "A demo, that'd be a tape of their own music?" he asked.

"Right."

"It sounds as though you and Bud were on good terms, if he discussed his music with you."

"I just listened in a bit when he was at the house discussing the 'business' with Hank. I figured it was dream talk, really."

"And when this tape's made, the next step is to get a manager?" She nodded.

Greg thought she was probably right. The boys would have some plan, however muddleheaded it might be. At least it gave him and Miss James some starting point in the way of places to look. "I'll pay a visit to the detective I hired and have him circulate the boys' picture at the studios where these demo tapes are made. There can't be that many of them."

"We can eliminate the bigger ones. They charge a fortune. I'm certain the group would go to little places. I can acquire that information from my friend. Nick works at a radio station," she added.

That helped explain Miss James's knowledge of the rock business, and maybe her outfit, too. She dressed to suit her Nick on the weekends. It must be very hard for her to masquerade as a businesswoman five days a week. But all that had nothing to do with him. "And there's the van," he said pensively. "The police can keep an eye out for it. I'll try to get in touch with Officer Levy. That's the man Waterloo sent down to help us look. He could tour the parking lots."

Jodie frowned in concentration. "Do you think they'd park it in a public lot? It costs so much in the city, and besides, the van might be broken into. It's carrying all their gear—thousands of dollars' worth. I bet it'll be parked as close as possible to wherever they're living. Maybe side streets and back alleys, places like that are where Levy should look."

"You're right, of course. Good thinking." Jodie felt a pleasant flush of pride. She hadn't expected Mr. Edison would be quite so generous with compliments. "The trouble is, I don't think like a kid," he added, robbing her of her moment's pleasure.

A kid! "Or a poor man. Someone like you thinks like a plutocrat," she said, but with a saucy smile, to take the sting out of it.

The blue eye that lifted suddenly to rake her held a spark of derision. "I wasn't born rich, you know," he said quietly. "I was once young, believe it or not. I can understand Bud's reluctance to get into the harness. I would like to have been a painter myself. Unfortunately, I had to earn a living."

"But you're—"

"Rich? I am now. It took a lot of work."

Jodie sat silent, thinking. She didn't know anything about Mr. Edison's background. She just assumed he had taken over his father's business.

"I'd like Bud to share the wealth, and the work, after he finishes Harvard." He could see she was surprised that he was a self-made man. He glanced at her, expecting a word of commendation, and was surprised to see the ironic set of her lips.

"Kind of you to share the wealth," she said coolly. It was that thoughtless *after he finishes Harvard* that annoyed her. "My own youthful folly was aspiring to become a ballet dancer," she added. Suddenly she wanted him to realize she had had a romantic dream, too.

He surprised her. "Any luck?" he asked, with apparent interest.

"No. I started studying too late. The instructors all told me that one has to start young. So I was forced to abandon my dream."

They discussed their plan as they drove into Toronto, through traffic that was already thick with commuters. The sun in their eyes made driving difficult in spite of the sunglasses they both wore, but soon the needle of the CN Tower punctuated the skyline, with glass skyscrapers mushrooming around it, blocking the glare. The expanse of Lake Ontario sparkling in the distance held them captive as if they were seeing it for the first time.

Jodie always felt a rush of excitement when entering a large city. She liked visiting Toronto, but had no desire to live there. For her, home now was Waterloo, not far from where she'd grown up.

"I'll park the car at the hotel and use taxis," he said, as the traffic grew denser. "Driving in the city's more bother than it's worth."

"And the subway's so handy," she added, to remind him he wasn't thinking like a poor boy.

He acknowledged it with a quick, apologetic grin. "And cheap."

It was the first genuine smile she'd seen since this whole affair began. Mr. Edison should smile more, she thought. It removed that stuffy look. "If you call $1.10 cheap."

He left the car at the entrance to the hotel for the car valet to park, and they went into the glittering lobby of the Royal York. He didn't say anything, but he couldn't suppress one uncertain look at Jodie as she walked along beside him. They made an incongruous pair, but worse, a suspicious one. He was too young to be her father, and their coloring was so different that they didn't look like brother and sister. Certain minds might infer he was robbing the cradle.

Her sneakers made a squeaky sound on the marble floor. It had been easy to forget how she was dressed when he was driving. Her conversation was mature and even intelligent. But now she looked nothing like the woman who'd masterminded their game plan to find the boys.

Jodie caught the glance and felt a surge of anger. "Don't worry. They're used to odd couples in Toronto," she said. "And besides, nobody will know you. I'll wait in the coffee shop. We don't want the desk clerk to think we're shacking up." She'd hoped to shock him by her blunt language, and when he showed no visible signs of agitation, she was disappointed.

His relief at her suggestion, however, was perfectly obvious. "I'll take your bag upstairs," he said.

She handed it to him, then strode angrily to the coffee shop. She caught a reflection of herself in the mirror and was moved to admit that she did look out of place in a swanky hotel like this, especially with Mr. Edison. A few heads turned to look at her. The Royal York was very staid, traditional, elegant. A place in which Gregory Edison would feel right at home.

The shop was busy with customers. An enticing aroma of coffee and bacon hung on the air, reminding her that her breakfast had consisted of one orange. She ordered coffee and a Danish, and had finished the pastry by the time Mr. Edison arrived. His dark head stood out among the crowd that had formed, waiting for a table. She admitted reluctantly that he was good-looking, in a formal, conservative kind of way.

She stood up and beckoned to him, and he joined her, trying not to show that he felt uncomfortable in her company. "Shall we dash, or do I have time for a coffee?" he asked.

"It isn't eight o'clock yet, Mr. Edison. We have time."

Mr. Edison bit the bullet and suggested something that he was afraid he'd regret, after this episode was over. At work, the formality of Mr. and Miss was strictly maintained, but here it seemed absurd. "My name's Greg," he said. "While we're here, there's no need to be formal."

"Mine's Jodie," she returned. She didn't fail to notice the remark, *While we're here*. Did he think the walls would cave in if she called him Greg at work? Old stuffed shirt!

Jodie joined her companion in ordering another cup of coffee, then they planned their strategy. "I'll get in touch with Levy and Palmer—Palmer is the private detective I hired—before they leave for their day's work," Greg said. "I have the number where Levy's staying, as well. He phoned me last night, and I told him I'd call him there this morning. I thought you and I might cruise around Queen Street by cab until things get moving. With luck we might spot the boys, or Bud's van."

Jodie didn't plan to spend the day with him, and objected immediately. "We should split up. That way we can cover more ground. I plan to go down to the radio station to see if I can get a lead there. The deejays know all about the rock scene. I'll find out where SWAK's kind of music is played. The boys will probably hang out at the clubs at night, to hear the competition and meet the other musicians."

"But we have to keep in touch!" During the drive, Greg had reluctantly admitted that he needed her help.

"Oh sure. I'll call you. When will you be back here?"

"We might as well meet here for lunch. We have to eat. Or is this out of your way?"

"Why not eat on Queen Street? The boys have to eat, too. We'll sit by the window and scan the crowds while we lunch. Or better yet—let's meet at P.J.'s. Hank likes it. They give huge servings. I took him there once," she added. "It's where the kids from Waterloo go when they visit Toronto."

"A working lunch." He nodded, impressed with her dedication. He was getting used to the big ribbon around her hair. A radiant blue, it reminded him of Alice in Wonderland. It made her look youthful, innocent, but he knew from work that there was an intelligent woman hiding behind it, so he tried to accept it. "Where is P.J.'s?"

"It's right beside the Eaton Centre. Perhaps the boys might tour the mall, as well. They're kind of tourists, in a way, and it gets more sightseers than the CN Tower."

"All right. We'll do lunch at noon, at P.J.'s. I'll have to make some arrangement to keep in touch with Levy and Palmer as well."

"You could find out where they'll be, and arrange to phone them. That leaves us free."

"Right," he said, impressed again at her quick thinking.

They finished their coffee and Greg took another cup up to his room. Jodie went with him to learn whether Levy or Palmer had come up with anything, before she and Greg began their search. While he made his phone calls, Jodie repaired her hairdo in his bathroom. She felt a little strange about going to meet Nickie in such a juvenile getup, but when she told her why, her friend would understand.

"No news," Greg said, when he finished his phone calls.

Jodie picked up her big shoulder bag and headed for the door. "Shall we hit the pavement?" she said.

"We'll hire a cab. I can drop you off at the station before I go to Queen Street," he said, opening the door.

"The station's not far from here. I can walk."

They had to run to catch the elevator. There were other people in it, and Greg didn't say anything till they reached the lobby. "Wouldn't you like to go in the cab?" he suggested hopefully. He looked concerned, and she couldn't figure out what was bothering him.

"Why?"

"I just don't think a young lady should be on the streets alone. Isn't that why I came, to help protect you?"

"No, you came to help me look for the boys." Jodie frowned in confusion. Was he developing a father complex about her? She must have succeeded better than she hoped in looking like a teenager. "Don't let the hair ribbon fool you," she said. That seemed to be what he was looking at. "I'm not a kid."

"That's what worries me," he said softly. His dark eyes had traveled down to her T-shirt and jeans.

"In broad daylight!" she exclaimed, and laughed out loud. "Oh Greg, you really are out of it. See you at P.J.'s at noon. Better buy some earplugs," she added, and left. This time she was smiling. So he had noticed she was a woman! And one that might tempt a lecher. It was just as well Mr. Edison was a stick-in-the-mud, because she certainly didn't want to tempt him.

Greg stood in the gilt and marble and red plush lobby, watching her as she swayed enticingly away from him in her tight jeans, her blond hair swinging. It was hard to believe he was looking at Miss James. She probably thought he was an old crock, but any man with blood in his veins would be excited by the way she looked. He was not completely calm himself, and he didn't even like her. He watched in frustration as a middle-aged businessman turned to follow her with his eyes. After she'd made a fairly safe exit, Greg went out to get a taxi.

Jodie was just a small-town kid, when all was said and done. She might have a sophisticated boyfriend living in Toronto, but she obviously didn't know much about men if she didn't realize how much of an attractive nuisance that outfit really was. Maybe she did realize it. Maybe it was to impress Nickie. She'd be meeting him at the station. Was that the reason she didn't want her boss tagging along?

After giving the driver his instructions, Greg settled back in the taxi, carefully scanning the streets as he went. They seemed to be full of groups of young men, in twos and threes. Were they all wayward youngsters who had run away from home? Why had Bud done it? He had given Bud everything money could buy. A fine house, and he even had his own wheels. He shouldn't have let him get the van. He should have insisted on the compact car, but no, Bud wanted the old wreck of a van. Now he knew why—to carry his equipment when he ran away.

Greg couldn't understand why a kid from a good home would toss it all away to go and live like a pauper in some hovel, so he could play that awful, loud music at night in some ratty bar. Bud was only twelve years his junior. How could there be such a vast gap between them?

The truth was, he didn't know Bud at all. He'd been so busy earning money to support them that he'd never found time to get to know Bud's deeper secrets. When he was home, he was studying. Once he finally graduated and got his first job, he had to work hard at it. Maybe by then they had already grown apart a little. Then when he started his own business, that consumed all of his extra time, but it had all been for Bud. All the saving for his expensive education...

He could remember himself at twenty-two, when the worst of the struggle was over. He had dreaded the thought of settling down to the dull routine of business after university. He had never cared that much about music, but he had once aspired to be an artist. He had given up that dream for Bud, and this was the thanks he got. The boy was willing to throw away an opportunity to come into the family business, starting at ground level. He couldn't let him do it. Bud didn't know what he was getting into. A man had to have a good job, a reliable career.

Music and art were marvelous, but as careers they were too chancy. Maybe Bud lacked the necessary creative genius to make a go of it. He'd be better off in business management. He'd enjoy it once he got settled in, as he himself enjoyed it.

He didn't forget to keep an eye on the streets as these thoughts drifted through his mind. The deteriorated area of small shops and dry cleaners and rundown houses, many of them with signs in the window advertising rooms to let, depressed him. It especially depressed him to think Bud preferred this to his own home. After he had toured Queen Street twice by taxi, he got out and began tracing the side streets leading off from it on foot, looking down alleys, peering into garages and finally stopping for a coffee, to rest his weary legs. There wasn't a single business suit in the little diner. Even in his shirtsleeves, he felt overdressed.

The crowd here was like something out of a futuristic masquerade ball. There were Mohawk haircuts, and heads of hair dyed red, green and blue, all on the same head. There were girls in skirts dragging the ground; others wore very short skirts with skimpy semimatching tops that revealed more than they concealed. They wore metal bracelets that clanked and rattled. Some of them had donned more jewelry than clothes. He had never seen anything like it; furthermore he hoped never to again. It was bizarre and unsettling.

Jodie's morning was more fruitful. She and Nickie Sommers went to the cafeteria and spoke with some of the deejays. Although Nickie worked at a rock radio station, she was all business. She wore a tailored dress and had her black hair cut in a short, sleek coif. In her case glasses were necessary. Nickie had always been shortsighted. She sported a very stylish pair of big, wire-rimmed glasses that made her blue eyes look even lovelier than usual.

The deejay who proved to be most helpful was called Ron Almont. He played in a rock group as well, which provided a closer affiliation with the local groups than his regular job did.

"What kind of stuff does SWAK play?" he asked Jodie.

"Pretty much middle of the road. Sort of jazz rock, like Hall and Oates. Which clubs feature bands who play that kind of music?"

Ron drew her up a list of the clubs and groups, and included names of the small studios that would make a demo tape at a decent price. "I could give you the names and addresses of some MOR group members, but it wouldn't do you any good," he said. "They wouldn't rat on other musicians. Half of them are runaways. They stick together."

"Right. I couldn't tell them why I'm here," she agreed. "I was thinking I might pose as a hopeful singer." She looked for Ron's reaction.

He appeared dubious. "They usually dress kind of funky. Can you sing?"

"A little," she said tentatively.

"A little! She performed a great rock number at our class concert," Nickie said.

"Roar Shock's looking for a female singer," Ron said, examining her carefully. "If you auditioned for them, you could casually ask if SWAK's in town. Don't say who you are, but you could say you're from Waterloo—that you know the guys. You might learn something."

Jodie felt a tremble to think of the ordeal of that audition, but it just might work. "Perfect! Thanks, Ron. I was hoping for something like this. Where can I reach the group?''

He wrote it out for her. "Oh, I thought it was Rorschach, as in the inkblot test," she said with a laugh. "Roar Shock—sounds like a heavy metal group," she said doubtfully.

"A stupid name. They're working on a new one," Ron said. "The guitar player was a psych student. At least he didn't call the group the Inkblot Test. The man in charge is Gary Delaney."

"Is it safe to go unescorted?"

"Yeah, they're cool. They don't do drugs or have any trouble with the police," Ron assured her. "They party after their shows, but they won't be drinking during rehearsal."

"I'll give Gary a call and try to set up an audition. Where do they practice?"

"They have a rehearsal hall in Etobicoke, in the suburbs. You'd better arrange for Gary to meet you. Oh, by the way, if you can't reach them, they're playing at Ruby's tonight. It's a small club at the corner of Queen and Soho. You could catch them there and give a listen to their stuff."

"I'll do that if I can't get in touch with Gary. Thanks, Ron, this is a real help. I have to run, Nickie."

"I brought you a spare key for my apartment," Nickie said, giving it to her then. "Just make yourself at home if I'm not there. I may be tied up tonight."

Before she left, Jodie gave Ron one of the pictures of SWAK, and described the boys in some detail. Two dark-haired boys and one blonde weren't an unusual combination. She feared they'd be easy to overlook, or forget. None of them was extra tall or short, or had any distinguishing marks. Ron asked if they'd be wearing T-shirts with their band's name on them, as some of the groups did for self-promotion. They hadn't had shirts like that when they left home, but she added the shops that put names on T-shirts to her list, and left.

Since Greg was scouting Queen Street, Jodie decided to spend the rest of her morning touring busy Yonge Street, the main street downtown. She stopped at any store that she thought might conceivably attract Hank and the others. She struck up conversations with the store clerks and young customers with no trouble. No one remembered having seen the boys, when she flashed the picture. Eventually she worked her way toward the Eaton Centre. It was in the right direction, close to P.J.'s, where she'd be meeting Greg Edison for lunch.

She walked the entire length of the mall, checking out the record and poster shops, T-shirt shops and refreshment stalls. She soon grew tired, her feet were hot from the heavy socks. Spotting a bench, she sat down beside the big fountain and just looked at the passing throng. Deciding she'd get a better view from above, Jodie went upstairs to look down over the railing. With high school just out for summer vacation, the place was thronging with teenagers. A dozen times she saw trios of young men lounging along, pushing one another and fooling around, but each time she realized they were strangers. After a while they all began to look alike.

It was nearly noon. She was tired and frustrated and becoming depressed. With fifteen minutes to kill before lunch, she decided to phone her mother, hoping that by some miracle Hank had called home. It took a while to gather the correct change. Her next challenge was to find a free phone that worked. She tried to sound cheerful, after learning that Hank hadn't surfaced, telling her mother she was working on some leads.

When she arrived at P.J.'s, Greg was just getting out of a taxi. He looked hot and tired and frustrated. They said hello, and went inside. The restaurant was spacious, and crowded with teenagers. Music was blaring so loudly you couldn't hear yourself think. Greg winced when they walked in, and Jodie's head throbbed with every beat of the music. She was suddenly sorry she had recommended the place.

"Let's do a quick search of the tables and leave," she suggested.

The relief on his face was obvious. "I see why you recommended earplugs," he said. Of course their tour showed them the boys weren't there. They hadn't really expected it would be that easy.

"Eaton's has a nice restaurant," she said. "It's close."

"We were going to tour the Centre anyway, so it's handy."

"I've already toured it once, but we'll look again."

They went to the restaurant in the big department store. It was crowded, too, but not raucous. This establishment attracted the business crowd and shoppers, so it had just the right ambience to make Jodie and Greg feel comfortable.

"I'm going to have a nice, cold beer and give my feet a rest before I eat," she said. "I thought sneakers would be comfortable, but in this heat… Of course with jeans I could hardly wear heels."

"Why did you feel you had to wear jeans?" he asked, trying not to make it sound like a complaint.

"I was planning to pose as a rock music fan, to make it easy to strike up conversations with the rock set."

Greg had a fleeting memory of the bizarre crowd he had seen in the coffee shop, and felt a twinge to think of Jodie consorting with such people. Her answer made him realize she didn't normally dress like this, even away from work.

"Judging by what I saw on Queen Street, you're underdressed. I wonder why the kids dress so weirdly," he said pensively.

"Music and clothing have always been ways for kids to show their rebellion. Don't ask why they rebel. You must remember that."

Greg had to think about it a moment. He had never rebelled, and his load had been heavier than most youngsters'. "To establish their own identity, you mean? To announce to the world that they're independent beings?"

"That's the way I remember it. You have to be cool, one of the gang." She wondered if Greg had ever been one of the gang.

"Flocking together is for sheep," he said dismissively.

She studied him discreetly, from the corner of her eye. Yes, he certainly seemed the independent type. Maybe he thought he was a little better than the others. Maybe he *was* better, she admitted reluctantly. His way had certainly succeeded for him, at any rate. When she noticed him gazing at her, she said offhandedly, "Different strokes for different folks, huh?"

She didn't want him to think her choice of clothing was a clue to her personality and added, "I thought I might pose as a teenager just out of school, trying to get a job singing with a rock band, as an in with the rock group."

"Sing with a rock band?" he exclaimed, staring in disbelief. "Trust me. You don't want to do it. You'd never fit in. Forget it," he said firmly, remembering the punks he'd seen that morning.

Jodie's temper rose at the commanding speech. "As a matter of fact, I'll be auditioning for Roar Shock in the near future," she said, as if it were an everyday thing. "It's a new band that's looking for a female lead singer."

"Good Lord!" Greg said, and just sat staring at her as if she'd announced she was going to fly to the moon. He had one image in his head of Miss James, with her prim glasses and chignon and computer terminal, not this new person called Jodie, standing up with a rock band. He burst out laughing.

Chapter Three

Jodie felt a sensation that was becoming tediously familiar: annoyance. "Thanks for the vote of confidence, Greg. I never claimed to be Tina Turner, but I can sing a little."

Greg cleared his throat and said, "Sorry. We'll blame that one on fatigue and frustration, shall we? But why on earth are you doing this?"

"I told you, to establish contact with the music crowd. They'll never tell us anything if they know why we're really here. I have to seem nonthreatening. I'll tell them I'm from Waterloo, that I know the members of SWAK, and want to see them. I'll ask if they've met the band, or heard anything about them."

"I was afraid you'd gone native on me and decided to join the runaways." He grinned. "Roar Shock sounded so unlike Miss James." His playful glances measured her new persona against the old. Impersonating a singer didn't seem too farfetched for this impetuous young woman who sat across from him. When had Miss James become so daring?

Obviously, there was more to this woman than what met the eye. He saw her scowl, and it seemed a good time to change the subject. He grabbed the menus, then said, "Let's see what they have to eat."

They ordered veal Parmigiana and a salad. "About this audition, where will it take place?" Greg asked. He felt bad about his untimely outburst of laughter.

"According to my friends at the radio station, it'll be held at a practice hall Roar Shock rents in Etobicoke."

"Couldn't they come to my hotel room?" he suggested. He had an awful image of Jodie, surrounded by a crowd of unkempt men wearing black leather vests decorated with metal chains.

"They keep their equipment at the hall, which I'm sure would never fit in a hotel room."

"Couldn't they bring their guitars and drums—"

"You've never watched SWAK practice, have you?"

It wasn't meant as an accusation, but Greg was becoming sensitive about his lack of interest in Bud. "I can see the Royal York wouldn't go for that," he prevaricated.

"The equipment wouldn't begin to fit in the room. Besides, transporting the instruments would be inconvenient. That's why I have to go there."

"I take it Nick will be accompanying you?" One man hardly seemed to be enough protection against a whole group. Greg felt he should volunteer to go, too."

"I didn't ask Nick to go with me," she answered calmly, though she'd have to ask someone. Maybe Ron Almont. It would be nice to have a man along, just in case.

Greg stared as if she were insane. "You're not going alone!" It was a command, not a question.

Jodie realized that he was concerned for her safety, and didn't let his tone upset her. "Ron said the group members are all right. He's the deejay who told me about them."

"But what would a deejay's idea of 'all right' be?" he demanded. His angry eyes and ironic tone reminded her very much of her father's, when he had come to Toronto to take her home. She had quaked with fear then, but she wasn't a kid now, and Greg Edison wasn't her father.

"They're all right," she answered, as if it were the most ordinary thing in the world for her to go alone to a rock band's studio.

"I believe sex is the prime item on the rockers' agenda. Sex and drugs and rock and roll. I can't let you go alone."

Jodie had mixed emotions about that speech. Despite her vexation, she really did want someone to go with her. Not Greg, especially. She'd feel like a fool singing in front of her boss, when she had to go on working for him after this was over. She'd ask Nick or Ron to go with her.

"They'd never believe you had anything to do with the rock business. You just don't look the part," she explained.

Greg did her the courtesy of thinking about her objection, but soon overcame it. "There must be businessmen involved in making music. The kind of money the record industry generates, there have to be businessmen. You mentioned our boys would be looking for a manager. I'll pose as your manager."

"But you don't know anything about the business," she pointed out.

"I know a lot about business. It's my specialty," he countered.

"Not the music business."

"Business is business. I'm a fast learner. You can fill me in on the details," he said simply.

"I haven't a clue about the business end of it," she admitted.

They exchanged a helpless look of mutual acknowledgement that they were babes in the woods in this area.

"The Roar Shock group—they aren't established," Greg said. "They can't be that savvy themselves. It stands to reason if they want to hire you, you'd either be on a salary or get a share of the profits."

"I don't think an unknown group could afford a salary, do you?" she said, more at ease discussing the rational, business side of the affair.

"That's true. We'll ask for a percentage of the performance fee, the same share as the musicians get. We'll insist on gross, the net's too easy to rig."

"That sounds fair. I doubt if it'll ever come to that anyway, once they hear me sing," she said. "And I don't even have the job yet. Perhaps Nick or Ron will agree to go with me. We'll see."

He lifted his brows and said, "Yes, we'll see, but you don't go alone, Miss James. Notice I've reverted to your professional name, to intimidate you."

His smile was far from intimidating. Jodie felt herself smiling in response. Since he had a sense of humor, maybe she'd let him tag along. "But would you respect me after, once you'd seen me belting out rock music?" she asked.

"I don't see why singing should affect your brain. And your having the ingenuity to pose as the enemy certainly wouldn't lessen my respect for a very competent worker. On the contrary, I admire initiative."

Jodie was pleased at his playful compliment. "They're not really the enemy," she said. "I like ballet. You like art, Bud likes music. Not all Edisons can invent the light bulb, you know. Why won't you allow Bud to attend Juilliard?"

"Juilliard?" he asked in astonishment. "He'd never get accepted there. It's this idea of forming a rock band that has to be stopped."

It was Jodie's turn to be astonished. "Didn't you know he was accepted at Juilliard?"

"Accepted?" He gave her a disbelieving look. "He didn't even apply."

"Yes, he was accepted! I saw the letter. He was so excited when it came, he ran right over to show Hank. But the acceptance from Harvard had come the day before. He had quarreled with you.... I guess he didn't even bother telling you," she said, in a small, sad voice.

"Good Lord!"

Jodie had often heard of the blood draining from someone's face. She had thought it was an exaggeration, but that was exactly what happened to Greg. He visibly turned pale. His dark eyes, glowing in his pale face, told her he was deeply shocked.

"I guess you two weren't very close," she said, not accusingly, but he read a reprimand in the words.

"Not lately," he admitted. "We used to be closer, when he was younger. Teenagers are naturally rebellious—well, we discussed that already. We've grown farther apart—a fact I'm not very proud of. I've been so busy at work, and Bud always seemed to be happy enough in his own life. The truth is, I took time to do the necessary scolding, but didn't really stop to just talk to him as a friend. You just assume your brother's your friend. He never once mentioned Juilliard to me, though he's kept up his piano lessons. I had no idea...." He shook his head, and fell silent.

Since Greg's concern appeared genuine, Jodie felt a little sorry for him. She knew something of the family background from Bud, and realized that Greg had carried a heavy burden in raising his brother. "I think most kids are closer to their moms," she said, to assuage his guilt. "I know I was. But I was sure he would have told you a thing like that. I mean, it meant so much to him."

This thoughtless ending made him feel even worse. It showed Greg clearly how far apart he and Bud had grown. Not wanting to be too lenient, he had gone in the other direction, and been so strict that Bud had hidden the really important aspects of his life. Education seemed vital to Greg, and he had pushed Bud pretty hard to do well in school. He had nagged at the way Bud styled his hair, and criticized the clothes he wore, probably a carryover from more youthful days. But Bud was no longer a kid. He was out living a life that his own brother had been unaware of. Greg had known that Bud played in a band, but when he came home late, he'd never asked how the playing had gone. He just lectured him for slacking off on his studies.

He had tried, from time to time, to have those heart-to-heart talks that fathers had with their sons, but Bud would turn sullen and uncommunicative. The memory of that sulky face still angered him, or perhaps the anger he felt had become a smoke screen, camouflaging his guilt. "I don't see why he was so damned secretive," he said with a scowl.

"Anyway, all this isn't going to help us find them. I'll have to get to a phone to get in touch with Gary Delaney. He's the head of Roar Shock. I was told his group's playing at Ruby's Tavern tonight. If we don't find the boys this afternoon, we should go to Ruby's tonight, and to some of the other MOR places. I have a list."

"MOR?" he asked, frowning.

"Middle of the road. It's the kind of music SWAK plays."

"SWAK! MOR. I don't see why they can't speak plain English," he said irritably. In his mind, he kept harping on Bud's keeping secrets from him.

Jodie shrugged her shoulders. "Every occupation has its own jargon. I don't suppose dividend tax credit and gross fixed-capital formation mean much to some people."

For one fleeting moment, he smiled. It was the incongruity of hearing such formal terminology coming from the ragamuffin sitting across from him. There was a ludicrous side to this entire business that would have amused him, if it had been happening to anyone but himself.

"Objection noted. I thought you were talking about the Dow-Jones when you first mentioned that deejay," he admitted. "Since we both have to use the phone, we might as well do it from the comfort of my hotel room, and give our feet a rest. There's no point cruising the streets all day. The odds aren't very good of bumping into the boys that way."

Jodie was no longer afraid that Greg would try anything in the privacy of his room. For one thing, he was pretty shaken up that Bud hadn't told him about Juilliard. She thought he was brooding about that. And for another thing, he was just as anxious to find the boys as she was. He definitely didn't have anything else on his mind. "Okay," she said.

They finished lunch and took a taxi to his hotel. The first thing Jodie did when they reached his room was to sit down on the desk chair to pull off her sneakers and socks. The thick socks were burning her feet. "These things are murder," she said, when she saw Greg watching rather closely. He was looking at her ankles. She felt like a Victorian lady, caught in an indiscretion.

"Did you pack any open shoes in that gunnysack you brought?"

"It isn't a gunnysack! You make me sound like a hobo or something. Everybody uses soft-sided luggage these days." Greg glanced at his hard-walled leather suitcase, but didn't say anything. "Everybody except bosses," she added, and yanked off the other sock.

"Can I give you a hand there?" he offered.

"Sure, offer to help after the job's done. I'm just going to use your bathroom to change into a cooler shirt, if that's okay?"

It was on the tip of his tongue to say, the offer still stands. What was happening to him? He had to remember this was an employee.

Jodie saw the flicker of mischief in his eyes, saw it turn to indecision, then consternation. But she couldn't figure out what accounted for it. Surely changing your shoes in front of a man wasn't considered suggestive behavior. There was a moment of conscious silence, then she said, "Why don't you just make your phone calls, and I'll leave to change in private without shocking you."

A teasing grin curved his lips. "Too late. I'm already shocked, Miss James."

She shrugged. "You shock easily. Sorry about that."

"It's not your fault. I shocked myself."

She was glad he turned toward the phone as he spoke. She wouldn't want him to see the question in her eyes. It was beginning to look very much as though Mr. Edison had a libido beneath his robotized business veneer.

Greg had arranged to phone Levy and Palmer at one. He made his calls while Jodie changed in the bathroom. Her cooler, short-sleeved T-shirt was cropped at the waist to let the breeze in. It was far from immodest, but when she moved, it crept up enough to show an inch of torso. Would that shock him, too? she wondered. She rooted in her knapsack for a pair of low-heeled sandals. They were gold, with laces tied Grecian-fashion around her ankles. She rolled up the cuffs of her jeans for extra coolness, then went back into the bedroom.

Greg listened to the men's reports, then gave them instructions to continue their search. Palmer was visiting studios that made demo tapes for small groups. Levy was going to tour the music stores, in hopes that the boys would eventually show up there.

Jodie, listening, threw in, "And the T-shirt stores. That's the kind of place where they're likely to go."

"Can I look now?" he asked, slowly turning around. His eyes lowered to her ankles and feet. With her jeans rolled up, he had a clear view of her shapely ankles. He saw women's ankles every day, but the gold laces surrounding hers lent an interesting air. Then he lifted his eyes toward her shirt. This one was different; it was lightweight, and clung to her feminine body.

Jodie felt self-conscious with her boss scrutinizing her so closely. "Are you finished with the phone?" she asked brusquely.

Greg said something to Palmer and hung up. "Your turn," he said. He lifted the receiver again and held it out to her.

As she came toward him, he noticed the gentle swaying of her hips. When she moved, an inch of bare skin at her waist peeped out. It was paler than her arms and legs, pale and smooth and soft looking, like a baby's skin. Greg found himself wondering what it would feel like to touch her. Her body looked firm, well toned, but it would yield if a man held her in his arms. He tried to shake away the thought.

She saw the way he was watching her body, and felt uncomfortable. Then his eyes met hers; there was a glow in them. It created a new awareness, a new feeling. The tension grew as he stood, unmoving, watching her.

"Are you going to give me that phone, or are you planning to adopt it?" she asked, using a light tone to ease the tension.

"Be my guest," he said, and handed it to her. His voice was burred with emotion. He made himself move across the room, because if he stayed beside her, he knew he'd touch her in a way a boss shouldn't touch a female employee.

A bachelor had to watch himself in this liberated age. It was the reason he insisted on the formalities at his office. This way one could avoid complications, keep the inter-office relationships at arm's length.

The moment passed quickly, and Jodie forgot it as she made her call. There was no answer at Gary Delaney's number. "Ron didn't have his address, so I'll just have to keep calling back every half hour or so," she said. "But we don't have to waste the whole afternoon here to do it. I can call from pay phones. Let's tour the tatty Yonge Street strip, and of course the Eaton Centre."

"And the pawnshops," Greg added. "In the old movies, musicians pawned their instruments when they were broke."

"SWAK wouldn't be that broke yet, but we can check around if we have time. They might have pawned their watches, I suppose."

"If Bud pawned the gold watch I got him for a graduation present, I'll crown him. He didn't seem to appreciate it much. I don't even own one myself."

"Poor thing, you have to make do with a designer model," she teased, pointedly adjusting her own inexpensive time piece. "And the reason he didn't appreciate it was because what he *really* wanted was a new pedal board for his guitar. He had already picked it out."

Greg didn't want to admit he didn't know what a pedal board was. Very likely Bud had been hinting for one, but if he had, Greg didn't remember. He held the door and Jodie slid past him into the hall. In her low sandals, her head came just to his shoulder. A wisp of blond hair tickled his chin. It smelled like a fresh meadow. Their hips brushed, and he felt a stirring of excitement. Had he positioned himself slightly in the doorway subconsciously so that she'd have to brush against him? he wondered. He wanted to take her arm, but Jodie was striding quickly toward the elevator, and the action seemed inappropriate.

"Shall we take a cab?" he asked, when they left the hotel.

"It might be a good idea. We have a lot of walking to do."

The doorman called a cab, and when she got in, Jodie casually put her big shoulder bag on the seat between them. She didn't really think it was necessary, but something had happened in the hotel. She no longer felt easy with him.

Every big city has its seedy area, and these few blocks of Yonge Street were Toronto's area of massage parlors and porno bookstores. Many of the pedestrians there matched the surroundings. Jodie found their search there a depressing experience, and she and Greg were both soon eager to leave.

"I feel soiled," Jodie said, wrinkling her nose. "I'm sure the boys wouldn't stay here long."

"Let's run, not walk, to the nearest exit," he suggested.

An intoxicated man approached with his hand out. Greg used him as an excuse to take Jodie's arm and pilot her along quickly. He was acutely aware of the feeling of her flesh beneath his fingers. When they had left the area, he casually let his fingers slide down her arm and clasped her fingers. Jodie didn't say anything or try to escape. She didn't want to make a big deal of it, but she was surprised, and constantly aware of his hand protectively clinging to hers.

At the Eaton Centre they turned east off Yonge and continued along Queen to Church Street, stopping at pawnshops. Greg showed his picture of the three boys, but if they had been in, no one remembered them. A vast array of guitars and saxophones and violins sat forlornly on the shelves, mute testimony to the hard time musicians had making ends meet. Jodie also found the trays of engagement rings and wedding rings made her sad. Did each of them indicate a broken marriage? Either a marriage or a death, she supposed. The shops smelled stale, and spoke of broken dreams. They were infinitely dreary.

Greg tried asking for a Rolex watch, and was shown a whole tray of them in three different shops. He checked the backs of some of the newer-looking ones. Jodie assumed he had had his gift to Bud inscribed. She was glad he didn't find what he was looking for. She knew it would hurt him if Bud had sold that watch. Greg obviously did care about Bud, in his own way.

"I should call Gary Delaney again," she said, after touring a few shops. She called him, and again there was no answer. They finished the row of pawnshops, finally giving up in frustration.

"It's good news, in a way," she pointed out. "They're not so broke they had to sell their instruments."

"Is your middle name Pollyanna, by any chance?" he asked. They turned and started back toward the Eaton Centre.

"No, it's Elizabeth. What's yours?"

"Ernest. Gregory Ernest Edison."

"That's a very—serious name."

"It makes it impossible to use a monogram. GEE!"

They came to a corner and Greg instinctively reached for her arm again. That time, it didn't feel strange to Jodie. It seemed natural when he later clasped her fingers and they continued strolling, like old friends.

"What'll you do when we find them, Greg?" she asked.

"First I'll give Bud a tongue-lashing, then we'll talk."

"Bud's eighteen. You can't make him come back, you know. I hope you talk him out of this idea though. Gil and Hank are only seventeen. We want Hank to finish high school, and Mrs. Turner feels the same way about Gil."

A quick frown pleated his brow. "You mean Bud's the oldest?" he demanded harshly.

"Yes. Didn't you know?"

"I just assumed they were all the same age. I had no idea the others hadn't even finished high school. I'm afraid Bud must be the ringleader. It was unconscionable of him to lead those kids astray."

"He's not much older," she pointed out. She didn't want Greg too angry at his brother. She hoped Greg would let

Bud go to Juilliard, but this didn't seem the time to push her idea.

The weather was beautiful in late June. In a cooler outfit, Jodie found the sun warm, without the heat stifling her. They were reluctant to leave the sunshine and go into the seasonless atmosphere of the mall, but that was next on their list, and when they reached the Eaton Centre, they went in. The place was always busy. It was bright and pretty, with a flock of sculptured geese perpetually poised in flight under the long raised glass roof. They looked so realistic you expected to hear them honk. Trees below gave the illusion of a natural setting. A vast fountain jetted water into the air.

They wandered along, stopping in stores selling records, posters or T-shirts, peering in or entering the shop if it was busy. They spotted dozens of boys who resembled Hank and Bud and Gil, but none were the three they so desperately wanted to find.

When they had completed the tour, Jodie made another phone call to Delaney. There was still no answer. "I don't know why he bothers having a phone when he's never there. You'd think he'd have an answering machine at least," she complained.

Greg looked surprised. "I can't believe it. Pollyanna's actually complaining. This is serious. It's time to stop for a drink."

Shoppers and students on holiday and retired elderly people crowded around them in the open restaurant. Jodie ordered an orange drink and sipped slowly, enjoying the cold drink on her parched throat.

Greg saw that she was tired and unhappy. Knowing it was his brother's fault made him feel guilty. His frustration was rapidly turning into a temper. "It was damned thoughtless of Bud to lure those youngsters into running away with him," he said grimly. "Your mother and Gil's must be hysterical. Kids so often don't go back and finish high school when they drop out.''

"And you had to leave town just when the McMurchy deal was closing, too," she added.

The McMurchy transaction didn't seem trivial to Greg, but it had assumed its proper place in the scheme of things. There were more important things in life than success and money. "I should phone the office. I forgot all about it." He was amazed that he could have forgotten it. This day was so different for him that it seemed unreal, but that other life was continuing, and it was important, too. "I'll have to run back to the hotel, Jodie. I left my papers there. There are a few things I want to check before I call the office. Will you come back with me?"

She considered it a moment. She would have welcomed the rest, but she remembered the way he had looked at her before, and decided against it. "No, I'll keep looking. I'm going to take the subway up to Yorkville. The boys couldn't afford to shop there, but they might have decided to have a look."

"You could use a rest. You're looking a bit fatigued," he said gently.

She was sure it was sympathy, and nothing else, that lent that glow to his eyes. "I want to strike while the iron's hot," she explained. "It's only been a day or so since they left. I might by chance, bump into them on the street. By tomorrow, I imagine they'll be working."

"I wish you'd take a taxi at least," he said, reaching for his wallet.

"The subway's faster. And who knows, they might be on the subway. I'll catch you later." She picked up her shoulder bag.

"You'll come back to the hotel?"

"I have to. My gunnysack's there. Will you be in your room?"

"Yes, I'll use it as an office. I have to speak to Levy and Palmer, too. I'll see you there in—what? An hour?"

"Maybe two."

He nodded. "Be careful."

She blinked in surprise. "Of what?"

His dark eyes traveled over her modest outfit. That one inch of naked flesh at her waist seemed to stand out like a beacon. "Mashers."

She laughed and walked off, already an object of interest to two leering young men. Greg added another black mark against Bud for involving Miss James in this imbroglio. Except that Jodie didn't seem much like the Miss James of Edison. She was much more—interesting. He shook himself to attention. The McMurchy case! He left.

Chapter Four

Jodie realized as soon as she entered the posh Yorkville shopping mall that the boys wouldn't spend two minutes there, amid the elegant jewelry boutiques and couturier clothing stores. It was a waste of time, but she was drawn by the merchandise and lingered awhile, peering in at windows. One of the shops had a half-price sale, and she was lured in by the hopes of a bargain.

As soon as she saw the dress on a mannequin, she knew she had to have it. It was a sea-green drift of chiffon, with narrow straps and a flaring skirt. She didn't know where she'd ever wear it, unless a miracle occurred and someone invited her to a dance at the country club. She glanced warily at the sale ticket and winced. Even at half price it was twice what she usually paid.

"What size is it?" she asked the saleslady who deigned to approach her. The clerk gave her a doubtful look. Jodie had already noticed the other shoppers wore chic, fashionable outfits. She half hoped the dress would be the wrong size.

It was her size. "Could I try it on?" she asked.

The clerk mentioned the price, as though to say, Beyond your range, dear.

"I know what it costs," Jodie said coolly.

The clerk looked pained, but she removed the dress from the mannequin. Jodie took it as though it were a rare objet d'art and went into the dressing room. It felt cool and luxurious as it slid over her heated body. One pull at the zipper and the dress closed around her like a second skin, as though it had been designed especially for her. It clung revealingly to her high breasts and small waist, and billowed out in a ruffle of crimped chiffon below. It felt like waves caressing her legs.

She hated to take it off, but knew she was wasting time, and hastened out of it. The clerk looked astonished when she said she'd take it. She examined Jodie's credit card as though it were a counterfeit bill, but the machine verified it, so she had to accept it. She placed the dress in a shiny black box with a silver rose embossed in one corner. Even the box was beautiful.

Jodie rushed out of the shop, juggling the box and her shoulder bag. She felt sinful for having indulged in shopping at such a time. She left the mall and went around the corner to the vintage clothing stores. They were interesting to her, but the boys would find them a dead bore. After a while, she took the subway back to the hotel. It was getting late, and the subway was crowded.

When she reached the hotel room, Greg met her at the door with a glass of cold beer in his hand. He looked happy to see her. "No news, I suppose?" she asked. He just shook his head.

"Same here. No sign of the boys at Yorkville. Is the McMurchy deal okay?"

"It's successfully closed. That's why I'm celebrating. I have a few bottles on ice, hoping you'll join me."

So it was business that made him look so joyful, and not her return. "A beer sounds great, just about now." She felt foolish with her dress box, and smiled to hide her embarrassment. "I know shopping seems inappropriate at this time, but I came across an irresistible sale—designer labels at half price."

Her green eyes glowed, and her smile was like a ray of sunshine. Already relieved by the successful closing of the deal, Greg felt his spirits soar higher. "Shopping's like breathing for a woman, or watching baseball for a man. Appropriate at all times," he said, while getting her a beer. He found her feminine folly delightful. He wouldn't have expected it of Miss James, but it seemed entirely appropriate to Jodie. When had she become two distinctly unique women? Not just a dual personality, but two entirely different women? He removed the bottle cap and handed her the bottle.

She lifted it, then clinked it against his. "Congratulations on the McMurchy deal, Mr. Edison," she said, and they drank.

"Mr. Edison? Why the formality?"

"I guess it was mentioning work that made it slip out."

"We're not at work now. Do I get to see the dress?"

She was surprised that he asked, and also reluctant to show it to him. Clothing was personal. You didn't show your new dress to a boss. "I'd better give Delaney another ring," she parried. "No word from Levy or Palmer?"

"They reported. They're carrying on, but there's no news."

She went to the phone. "This is an expensive way to call—from your room. They really charge you," she felt obliged to point out.

"McMurchy will pay for it," he said, smiling inwardly at her thrift. He was far enough removed from poverty now that the cost hadn't occurred to him. A woman like Jodie probably had to be a little careful about money. Was that why she was staying with Nick, because she couldn't afford to pay for a hotel room? He should have offered to pay! This whole mess was Bud's fault.

"Still no answer," she said, hanging up the phone.

"About your staying with Nick, Jodie," he said, rather tentatively. Money would be a sensitive point with her, but Nick, the deejay, was becoming a sensitive one with Greg. Something inside him turned hot and fierce when he thought of it.

"That's all arranged. I have a key."

He wondered how long she'd had it. She didn't say she had just received it that day. Greg watched her with narrowed eyes. "I see. Then I don't suppose it would do any good to suggest you stay here instead." Jodie emitted a gasp of surprise. "In a separate room, I mean. Naturally." He frowned, to cover his embarrassment, and hurried on with his reason, or excuse. "It would be more convenient in our search, that's all. I'd be happy to pay, if—"

"No!" It came out loud, almost vehement.

"Nick would object, would he?" His dark eyes bored into her. They seemed to be implying more than his actual words. They were keenly interested, perhaps worried.

She decided to tell him the truth, and either kill his interest, or set his mind at rest, depending on what he felt. "He? Niccola's my girlfriend," she replied, and took an unconcerned drink from her bottle. She mistrusted that satisfied little smile that flashed on his face and added, "I don't make a habit of staying with my men friends overnight. It might give them ideas."

Greg's smile congealed, but he went on looking at her. She returned stare for stare. And that goes for you too, boss, the look said. "I meant separate rooms," he said brusquely.

"So you said. I should phone home. Mom must be on tenterhooks."

"A good idea." The prickly moment passed.

She called her mother. Greg, overhearing the conversation, smiled at her way of delivering bad news. She didn't mention the depressing, futile search, but said they were beginning to meet people who were sure to know where the boys were. She was a thoughtful daughter, wanting to sound hopeful and to reassure her mother, when she must be frustrated herself. A smile moved his lips when she lowered her voice and murmured, "Yes, he's very helpful. Yes, Mom. I *know* he's my boss."

She cast a quick glance at Greg, and saw him grinning at her. She lifted her hand, crossed her fingers and said, "Oh yes, he seems to know just what to do. I'm sure he'll find them soon. Bye." Then she hung up.

"Do you make a habit of lying to your mother, Jodie?" he asked.

"I didn't see any point in worrying her."

"You make me feel like a dolt. I *should* know what to do."

"Why should you?" she asked, sitting on the side of the bed. "This is all even stranger to you than it is to me."

Greg sat on the desk chair across from her. "I should have listened to Bud more closely."

"You're only human. You had no way of knowing he'd run away." It seemed strange to be comforting Mr. Edison, who never seemed to want or need comfort from anyone. He always seemed so self-sufficient at work, almost cold really. Some people wore a mask like that. She supposed he must have been quite young when he actually started the company. Maybe he'd assumed his veneer to give him confidence with his employees. But surely he could relax a little by now.

"I never claimed to be Superman," he said.

"No, you just acted like him."

He frowned. "What do you mean by that?"

"I guess Superman was the wrong word. I just meant cool, in charge. Maybe a little—unfriendly," she said uncertainly.

"I try to be fair."

"Oh, you are! I didn't mean you weren't. It's just…well at most workplaces now, people use first names. It's friendlier. There's more of a family feeling," she said, not quite satisfied with her explanation.

"I don't think of my company as a family."

"But you said you didn't really make a friend of Bud, either, and he *is* family. Who *are* your friends, Greg?"

"I have lots of friends," he answered swiftly, defensively. "The people I went to school with, other businessmen."

"Of course. I was out of line. Sorry."

"And I hope you and I are friends, Jodie," he added, with an uncertain look.

"I hope so."

This runaway scheme of the boys was having some very strange effects. Here she was, drinking beer with Mr. Edison in his bedroom, asking him personal questions that were none of her business, and instead of telling her to mind her own business, he was asking her to be his friend. Just twenty-four hours ago, it would all have sounded not only bizarre but impossible.

Greg was still curious about her new dress, but she didn't open the box, and he didn't dare press the point. It was none of his business anyway, but he was curious. A designer label didn't sound like Miss James. That glossy black box with the silver rose embossed on the side suggested some glamorous creation.

"I expect we should make a reservation for dinner," he mentioned, as they sipped their drink.

"I should give Nickie a call. She might have planned something, although the visit was totally impromptu."

No fierce fire burned in him now when she mentioned Nickie. "Why don't you do that? If she's busy, you and I can have dinner together."

Jodie felt she should ask him to join her and Nickie. It seemed rude not to since he'd be alone otherwise, yet she resisted the idea. Actually he and Nickie would probably get on like a house on fire. Was that why she didn't want to suggest it? She called the radio station, and reached Nickie just as she was leaving. "What are you doing for dinner?" she asked.

"I have a date, but you're entirely welcome to join us," Nickie said.

Jodie felt a decided sense of relief. It alerted her that she wanted that private dinner with her boss, in spite of the difficulties that might arise, or maybe even because of them. "Oh no, I won't crash in if you have a date. I just thought you might be free."

"What will you do?" Nickie asked.

Jodie looked at Greg, who was making a show of rifling through his briefcase, although she suspected he was listening. "I'm with a friend," she said. Greg looked up, barely able to control a little smile of satisfaction. He quickly lowered his eyes, but she'd seen it.

"Is he handsome?" Nickie asked eagerly.

Jodie let her eyes steal back to examine Greg. His dark head was bent over the case, but she'd already memorized the features of his face. "You might say that. So I'll see you later. Will it be inconvenient, my being on your sofa? I mean if you want to bring your date in . . ."

"Don't worry about it."

"Okay. See you later." She hung up. "Nickie has a date, so it looks like we're stuck with each other, boss," she said lightly.

Greg hid all his pleasure and replied blandly, "I'll make that reservation. Since you haven't gotten through to Delaney, we'll have to go to some of those rock places tonight."

"Yes, but we don't have to eat early on that account. I don't imagine they get lively until quite late."

"Then we won't have to settle for a quick hamburger or pizza. We can dine in style." Then he looked at her, as if to say, Where am I going to take you, in jeans and a T-shirt?

"It's too bad I didn't bring any decent shoes with me. Otherwise I could wear my new dress," she said.

His eyes slid to her feet, but lingered on her slender ankles, with the flirtatious gold straps. "What's wrong with the ones you're wearing? They're all right for summer."

"Not for my new dress," she objected. Silver, strappy sandals were what she pictured, or something light. Maybe a sling pump with a high heel. And Toronto would have a better selection than she'd get back home.

As if reading her mind, Greg looked at his watch and said, "The stores aren't closed yet. If you hurried..."

"I can't waste time shopping when we're supposed to be looking for the boys," she countered, but it was exactly what she wanted to do.

"We've done what we can, for the time being. We'll be on the job again tonight," he answered reasonably. "I don't see any harm in it, but I repeat, there's nothing wrong with those things you're wearing."

The very fact that he called them "things" confirmed that they weren't good enough. "There's a mall right under the hotel," she said, talking to herself. "If I hurried..."

"I'll make the reservation before we go," Greg said, reaching for the phone.

"No, it'll be...faster if I go alone," she said. Jodie didn't want her boss along while she was shopping. It seemed too intimate, and besides, he'd probably try to pay the bill.

"You're right. I'll shower while you're gone. That way the facilities will be free for you when you return."

"A good idea," she said. She picked up her purse and ran from the room. Showers! She hadn't even thought of that. Naturally they had to shower after being in the hot, muggy city all day. Now that was really intimate, and emotionally uncomfortable. At least she'd be out of the room while he showered; later, she'd invent some ruse to get rid of him while she showered and changed. She'd send him down for a newspaper.

The shoes weren't on sale, but they were so lovely that Jodie didn't mind paying the full price. She was torn between two pairs, but chose the more practical ones, silver sandals that she could wear with other outfits. She hoped Greg chose a fancy restaurant, or she'd be ridiculously overdressed.

When she got back to the room, Greg had showered and changed into a light summer business suit. The strange nature of this trip came washing over her, at seeing Greg looking like her boss again. In his suit and shirt and tie, and with his hair freshly combed, she found herself thinking of him not as Greg, but as Mr. Edison. Yet there was some change in him. It was his expression. He looked eager, happy to see her.

"I see you found some shoes," he said with a smile, glancing at the box.

"Yes."

"Good. I have to dash out and get a few things myself. I've found I came without clean socks for tomorrow. Will half an hour be long enough?"

That telltale question revealed his real reason for leaving. He was sensitive enough to realize it would be embarrassing for her, showering with her boss right outside the door. That was thoughtful of him. "That'll be fine," she said.

"Oh, I almost forgot! I got reservations here at the hotel. Is the Imperial Room all right? I was going to try the Mermaid, but I didn't know if you liked seafood."

"I love lobster."

"Then we'll try the Mermaid tomorrow night. Don't forget to wash your face. "You've got soot on your cheek." He smiled when he said it, and touched her cheek. It was a casual gesture, but strangely intimate. Yesterday, Mr. Edison would no more have touched her face than he would have danced a jig. He had definitely changed; the relationship had changed. Only a friend would touch you. And if they were still here all day tomorrow, what new changes might occur?

He left, and Jodie went into the bathroom. He had cleaned it so thoroughly you would never have guessed it had just been used. She looked in the mirror, and saw the speck of dirt on her cheek. She must have got it on the subway. She looked tired and disheveled. In fact, she looked awful.

Her hair was beginning to come undone. It hung in tousled disarray around her face. All day, Greg had been looking at this messy picture. This wasn't her. She always made it a point to be neat and tidy at work—businesslike. She could be better than businesslike for a couple of hours, and change again before they went to Ruby's.

The stinging needles of water were refreshing. They stirred her fatigued body back to life. After the shower, she wrapped herself in a towel and dried her hair, forming it in loose waves with the dryer. She applied a modest amount of lipstick and eye makeup, after which she felt much better about herself. It was really too bad that she had had to look so scruffy for most of their time together. Mr. Edison had seen her as a prim office worker, and Greg had seen her as a teenage rock fan. Now Greg Edison was going to see her as herself. She hoped that he didn't lose interest completely, because she was beginning to find him quite fascinating.

She slid into the sea-foam dress, wiggled into the silver sandals and was ready. It had taken her twenty-five minutes. For the next five minutes, she nervously paced the room. She finished her flat beer, because her throat was dry and it didn't seem worthwhile opening a new bottle. In exactly half an hour, there was a tap at the door, then Greg let himself in.

Jodie knew at his first glance that he hadn't lost interest. His eyes glowed with pleasure, and an anticipatory smile curved his lips, as he slowly examined her. "You were right. The dress deserved new shoes," he said. The low husky inflection in his voice, coupled with the way he looked at her, made it a grand compliment.

"I washed my face, too," she said, suddenly feeling shy under his approval. To bring the atmosphere down to earth, she asked, "Did you get your socks?" Only after the words were out did she notice how domestic they sounded, almost as though they were married. She looked away from Greg, because she thought the same thing had just occurred to him. It was the way he looked at her, with familiarity.

"Yes." He was carrying a bag, which he put in his suitcase, although she suspected those socks hadn't really been necessary. "Are you all set?"

"Ready and waiting."

They went to the elevator, feeling a tingle of excitement in the air. No one looked askance at them as they crossed the lobby this time. In the dimly lighted dining room candles flickered, creating an oasis of linen cloth and flowers. The maître d' showed them to a table and handed Greg the wine list.

"Our celebration definitely calls for champagne," he said. "I believe in celebrating life's victories—business coups, birthdays, anniversaries, graduations—not neces-

sarily in that order. We'll have a big wingding when we get
our boys back. Meanwhile, let's enjoy the McMurchy
triumph. It'll mean a few new employees, and pay raises in
some quarters.''

The champagne lent a happy mood to dinner, and Jodie
decided there was nothing wrong with forgetting about
Hank and Bud and Gil for a few hours. They shared a cha-
teaubriand, which the waiter flambéed at their table, lending a festive touch.

"What do you do when you're not programming your
computer, Jodie?" Greg asked.

"It depends on the season. I swim and play tennis in the
summer. Jog and ride my bike in spring and fall, ice-skate
in the winter. How about you?"

"I swim and golf in the summer. We have a summer place
on Lake Huron. We go up there when we can get away, just
weekends mostly. I ski on the weekends in the winter. Bud
likes that, too. I usually take my vacation in the autumn. I
love traveling then. I took Bud to Europe once, but he didn't
really appreciate it. He stays with relatives while I'm away.
I like to get to those marvelous galleries in Europe as often
as I can. They're less crowded in the fall. I'm going to Spain
this year. I haven't really seen much of the Prado."

Greg's thoughts were on Bud as he spoke. Had he abandoned Bud too much? Maybe he should have insisted on
taking Bud with him on those European vacations. Those
places were really crowded in summer, though, and in autumn, of course, Bud couldn't go.

Jodie was thinking of something else. Greg led a more
glamorous life than she did. It emphasized the differences
between them. She suddenly felt insignificant and inexperienced. She must have been crazy. What would a sophisticated, wealthy man like Greg Edison want with her? Their
worlds were leagues apart.

"Have your been to the Prado?" he asked.

"No. I visited the Louvre when I was in Europe. I made one of those six-week, thirteen-country tours after I graduated," she said, not trying to make it sound grand.

"You don't really get to know the country that way, unfortunately. I prefer to spend two or three weeks in one country."

"So would I, if I could afford it," she said frankly. "But since I had never been abroad, and won't likely be going again for a few years, I wanted to see as much as I could. I'm not really keen on art, so I didn't spend a lot of time at the galleries and museums."

Sensing some hostility beneath her words, Greg changed the subject before she accused him of being a capitalist. "Do you find much time to read?" he asked. Reading seemed safe.

"Some. I prefer women writers, by and large. They're more likely to write about the kinds of things I'm interested in. I like Penelope Lively, and Fay Weldon."

Greg had obviously never heard of them. "I read mostly the male authors myself. Updike, Cheever..." He saw he wasn't striking any chords there and didn't continue.

"I don't suppose you watch much television," Jodie said. She didn't intend to make any claims to being an intellectual. There was no point in laying claim to knowledge she lacked. Most nights she was at home, watching TV with her mother.

Greg knew he wasn't imagining the animosity in her tone. She made her claim to watching television sound like a challenge. "On the contrary, I watch it a lot. It's relaxing after a day's work. PBS has some interesting programs."

She'd had a feeling he'd drag in PBS. "I find the sitcoms more relaxing," she said, although she liked PBS, too. She just wasn't going to pander to his interests.

"What got you interested in computers?" Greg finally asked, in desperation. The dinner date was deteriorating so quickly they'd soon be fighting, if he didn't find some common ground.

"They're the wave of the future. I wanted to get into something that would make me a good living. Besides I happen to like them a lot. They're so logical."

"Logic isn't usually considered a feminine virtue," he said provocatively.

"We're discovering new virtues every day, now that we're unchained from the stove," she riposted. "Computers are the greatest new technology since the automobile. They're changing the world just as radically as the car did in the early part of the century."

"They've certainly streamlined work in the business world," he said. But why did she sound so aggressive about it?

"That's just the tip of the iceberg. When every household has a terminal, all our shopping and banking will be done by computer, too."

"I thought housewives liked to tap the melons and squeeze the tomatoes," he said, trying for a light touch. "Or are your newly discovered virtues crowding out the old ones?"

"Merchants would soon learn that people wouldn't accept inferior merchandise. Lots of things could be done by computer, and look how it would cut down on traffic and pollution."

"I had no idea this brave new world was staring us in the face. It sounds like science fiction."

Jodie was soon carried away by her enthusiasm, and said, "Some futurists think the entire concept of leaving home to work in an office is obsolescent. I could do my job at home, if I had a modem to the office. It'd be a terrific reduction in overhead for you."

Relieved that he had finally found some common ground, Greg encouraged the conversation. . . .

"I remember a catastrophe at the office when we first went to computers. We lost some important files. Fortunately, we had hard copy, but it was a hair-raising moment."

"They overcame that long ago, Greg. You can get an uninterruptable power supply now. They had a little trouble with the horseless carriage at first, too, if you recall." She was actually smiling now. The candlelight flickered on her heart-shaped face, and made her hair look like moonlight. It was that cool, silverish blond, not golden.

"How old do you think I am?" he objected. "I wasn't around when the Model T was invented."

"You must have heard the rumor of trouble. Does the phrase 'Get a horse' ring any bells?" she teased.

"No. The first car that really caught my interest was the Barracuda. I was still in elementary school at the time. I'm not sure I like this new world you describe, where people are locked up alone, each in his little cubicle. It sounds like something out of *1984*."

"I thought you'd like it, since you don't take any personal interest in your employees anyway. Just kidding!"

"I take a keen interest in them," he defended. "What's more important, paying them a good wage and making sure their job is secure, or calling them Joe and Harry?"

"Paying them a good wage, but addressing your employees more informally would be a nice perk."

"Well, to tell the truth, when I first started my business it seemed impertinent to be calling men who were ten years older than I was by their first names. I guess formality just became a habit."

"Habits can be broken," she said lightly. "But I didn't mean to hassle you. We were talking about computers. If we worked at home, the work hours would be shorter. We'd have more time for R and R."

"It sounds decadent."

"You're fighting science, Greg. And your name is Edison," she said, shaking her head at his old-fashioned ideas.

"No relation to Thomas Alva, I'm afraid. Quite frankly, I'm afraid of the robots taking over the world."

"They can only do what we program them to do, but I admit I'm a fanatic on the subject. Let's talk about something else. If we can find a neutral subject," she added, with a laughing look. "I'm not an egghead, Greg. I don't read Schopenhauer for fun and relaxation."

"Who does? I've been known to watch the odd sitcom myself. It's the differences in people that are interesting. I'm afraid to even ask what music you like."

"That depends on my mood. What they're playing is nice for here, and now. What is it, do you know?"

"An Austrian waltz, I think. It sounds vaguely reminiscent of Strauss. And with Austrian music, we definitely have to have something with whipped cream for dessert. It's a feature of Austrian food," he added.

"Vienna was included in my tour. The Austrian pastries at Sacher's were sinfully delicious."

"I put on five pounds."

"I loved Vienna," she said with a nostalgic smile. Her green eyes took on a dreamy look. "We toured the wine country, stopped at some of the vineyards. We saw the Schönbrunn Palace, and the Lippizaner stallions. They seemed like clockwork horses to me, so unnatural. Vienna is one of my favorite cities. It's so romantic, the baroque architecture, the *platz*es and the people, so carefree."

Once Jodie overcame her pugnaciousness, Greg discovered that she had gained a great deal on her one tour abroad. She was by no means an uncultured hick, nor such a monomaniac about computers as she had led him to believe.

They lingered over a second cup of coffee, talking like old friends. Jodie hated to bring the evening to an end, but it was getting late, and it was time to go. Some people were just beginning to drift to the dance floor. But Jodie's audition lay ahead.

"It's too bad we have to leave," Greg said. Dining with Jodie was nice, but dancing would have made a good excuse to hold her in his arms.

"I still have to get into costume."

"Shall I meet you in the lobby?" he suggested.

"You can wait in the bedroom, if it's more comfortable." She had overcome that sense of strangeness that had bothered her before. She didn't mind if Greg was in the next room while she changed.

"I'll pick up a newspaper and wait in the lobby," he decided. He was eager to do what would make her comfortable.

"Ashamed to come down on the elevator with me, huh?" she joked.

"Not at all. In fact, it's preferable to being picked up in the lobby, which is probably what people will think."

"It's up to you." She shrugged.

"If you're sure you don't mind, I do have a few costume changes to make myself. I bought a couple of tin chains and a kerchief to hang around my neck, hoping to make myself look more like a musician's manager."

"You needn't have let on you needed clean socks." She grinned.

"So you guessed my strategy! The chains and the kerchief were a last-minute inspiration. There's ten bucks down the drain."

"Halloween's coming. You confessed at dinner that you like to celebrate all occasions. You can go as a hippie."

"And you can go as a flower child," he replied.

Where had the idea they'd still be seeing each other by the end of October come from? She felt a rush of pleasure at the thoughtless speech, but didn't want him to notice. "And waste my witch's outfit?" she joked.

"Do you really fool anybody, with that blond hair?" His eyes caressed it in a way that sent shivers up her spine.

Her voice was a little breathless when she answered. "That's stereotypical thinking. Who said blondes can't be witches?"

"Walt Disney," he replied promptly, and signed the bill that was placed in front of him. He helped Jodie with her chair and they left the restaurant. The emotional moment was gone, but a good feeling lingered. "Is it true blondes have more fun?" he asked as they left.

"You should have picked up a bottle of peroxide while you were buying your chains. Then you could find out for yourself."

"It's not necessary," he said.

"You enjoy life as a brunette, don't you?"

"Probably not as much as I should," he conceded. "But it seems to me a blonde can't have much fun by herself, and you're my date tonight. Some of the good times have to spill over on to me." He tilted his head and grinned, to show he wasn't suggesting anything untoward. "So far, it's been great."

Jodie didn't say anything, but she was inclined to agree with him.

Chapter Five

Jodie was sorry to have to resume the role of hopeful rock singer, just when she had been getting along so well with Greg. "Do you think I really have to change?" she asked, when they went into his room. She would not have worn the outfit to a club at home, but Toronto was a much bigger city.

"People wear anything here, to judge by what I've seen today," he replied.

"If we get a chance to meet Gary Delaney, I'll tell him we've been out to dinner. That'll explain it, if I'm over-dressed," she decided. "Are you going to change?"

"I'll leave my jacket behind. It's warm tonight." He removed his jacket and tie, opened the top buttons of his shirt, and was trying to decide about the chains and scarf. "What do you think?" he asked, holding them up for her inspection.

She examined his purchases and shook her head. "No, they're not you, Greg." He tossed them onto the bed, with an air of relief. She picked up her big shoulder bag and they left.

Jodie knew as soon as they arrived at Ruby's that it wasn't one of the more respectable clubs. It was on a run-down street, and the sign in front wasn't the familiar neon-lighted sort. It was just painted on the window, a diamond-shaped jewel done in red, with rays issuing from it, like a child's drawing of a sunset. A placard said, Roar Shock Playing Tonight.

Inside, the ambience was about what she expected—dark and noisy, with uncovered tables set close together. The place was three-quarters empty, so that finding a seat was no problem. She saw at once that both she and Greg were hopelessly overdressed, but it was dark, and maybe no one would notice. It didn't take more than a minute to see that the boys weren't there. People were still coming in, so they kept looking. At the front of the room, a raised stage held racks of amplifiers, microphones and a rat's nest of wires. Greg ordered two beers, then they sat, waiting.

Before long, the manager came out announcing, "The band you've all been waiting for—Roar Shock." A light ripple of applause greeted the group. The lead guitar had a frizzy curtain of burgundy-colored hair and wore a silver top, draped with scarves. The others wore black shirts and pants and high boots with silver stars glittering in the light.

"My God, is this what Bud wants to be?" Greg asked faintly.

"If Hank comes home looking like this, Mom'll disown him. This is probably just their stage costume. They wouldn't dress like this on the street," she said, to reassure him and herself.

The music was loud and the band played for what seemed an eternity. The music was accompanied by flashing red and blue lights, which were clouded by an occasional burst of smoke from dry ice. The numbers were interspersed with jokes and chatter of a fairly vulgar nature. Conversation was impossible while the band was playing, so Jodie and Greg just sat, looking at the door and listening. When the first set was over, Jodie said, "I'd better go around to their dressing room now, and see if Gary will talk to me."

Greg frowned, but that was why they had come, so he didn't try to stop her. He held her chair, and when they stood up, it seemed every eye in the room turned to them. They heard laughter, and some rude remarks.

"I didn't know Ruby's had become a yuppie heaven," one man said.

"Yuppies? You calling Princess Di a yuppie?"

They pretended not to hear. Greg followed Jodie when she went toward the stage. "I'll have better luck alone," she said. "Wait for me at the table." He was reluctant to let her go alone, but she insisted.

A man was adjusting the sound gear on stage, and she asked him where the dressing room was. He pointed to a door on the left. She went to it and found herself in a dark, narrow corridor. A few feet down the hall, loud talk and laughter came from an open doorway. She hurried to the door and tapped lightly. Inside, she could see the musicians opening bottles of beer, and wiping the perspiration from their brows. There were five or six women in the room, wearing the sort of clothes she felt she should be wearing. Black leather, short skirts, feathers in their ears. They were praising the band and smiling and making themselves agreeable.

A dead hush fell over the room when they spotted her. "Are you looking for Buckingham Palace, dear?" one girl said.

"Oh! A fashion show!" Another girl laughed. "You didn't tell me you had such high-class friends, Gary. I would have worn my mink."

Jodie looked around till she spotted Gary. She feared by the look on his face that she was in for trouble. His expression was something between amusement and derision. He raised his arm and beckoned her in. "Party time, doll. Grab a bottle," he said, while examining her from head to toe. He put an arm around her waist and drew her into the room.

"I really just wanted a word," she said in confusion.

He was older than he had looked on the stage. About Greg's age, she thought. To ingratiate herself with him, she said, "The show was fantastic."

"Glad you liked it."

Wanting to get out of there as soon as possible, she rushed straight into business. "I was speaking to Ron Almont about you today—the deejay at CDJM."

"Oh yeah, cool guy, Ron. You work at CDJM?"

"No, I'm looking for work. He said you might be interested in hiring a singer."

His eyes widened in disbelief. "I don't do opera."

She laughed gaily. "Oh, neither do I. Strictly rock and roll. Don't let the—the threads fool you. I'm just dressed up like this because I had to go to a boring old party."

He considered this, and seemed to believe it. "Who have you worked with?"

She invented a group on the spot. "Avro, from Waterloo. They do your kind of music. They just folded, and I came to Toronto."

"You came to the right place. Hey guys, meet—uh, what did you say your name is?"

"Jodie."

"Meet Jodie."

The band members came closer, eyeing her with avid curiosity. A front singer's appearance was as important as her singing. She set the image for the band. Although these group members weren't impressed by what they saw, to judge from their comments. "If we're switching to Broadway's greatest hits, count me out," one member said, with a satirical glance at the others.

"Broadway?" One of the girls laughed. "I thought she escaped from *The Ed Sullivan Show*."

Gary put an arm around Jodie's waist to lead her aside. "Don't pay any attention to them. Can you meet me after the show?" he asked.

"I thought I might meet you at your practice studio for the audition," Jodie said. She wasn't actually afraid, although she was beginning to get the idea that Gary was interested in more than her singing.

He inclined his head close to hers and said, "Sure, but let's talk and get to know each other a little first."

"I really should be going now. What time would be convenient—"

"No time like the present." He laughed, pulling her closer against him.

Jodie felt a tremble of fear shiver up her spine. She looked to the door, planning to make a run for it, and saw Greg looming in the doorway. He took one quick look at her in the clutches of Gary, and a scowl descended on his face. He looked ready to murder someone. A silence fell over the room.

"Who the hell is he?" Gary exclaimed. Greg was glaring at him with eyes that would have frozen fire. He strode into the room and took Jodie's hand. Gary released her.

"This is my manager," Jodie said in a weak voice.

"Greg Edison," Greg said, offering Gary his hand.

Gary took a mental inventory of Greg's appearance and assumed he was dealing with someone important. "Pleased to meet you, sir."

The talk and laughter resumed around them. "Why don't you join us at our table, Gary?" Greg suggested. "I've been enjoying your music. Maybe you and I can do some business."

"I can spare you five," Gary said, and they went out together. Greg ordered him a drink.

"So, you're Jodie's manager," Gary said. "I play strictly rock, you know."

"Yes, that's my line," Jodie said swiftly.

"Who else do you manage? Anybody I might know?" Gary asked Greg.

"You wouldn't know his clients. Greg's from the west coast," Jodie said, before Greg could put his foot in it by announcing some famous group. Lost as she was, she feared Greg was even more out of it.

"I'm looking to broaden my base. I plan to sign up a few Toronto bands," Greg said.

"We already have a manager. That might complicate things."

"Contracts are always negotiable," Greg said temptingly. "Of course you'll want to hear Jodie sing first. Shall we arrange an audition?"

"We didn't plan to hire a singer who's already under contract. I'd have to talk to my manager. Tell you what, folks, why not let Jodie join us for a number, then we'll see how it works out."

Jodie swallowed, and grasped at the first straw she could find. "The trouble is, I don't know your repertoire, Gary."

"No sweat. We'll play a cover tune."

"Oh, a cover tune," she said, in confusion, looking to Greg for help.

"Just what—er, cover, did you have in mind?" Greg asked.

Gary looked at them both with rising doubt. "You name it. I'm easy."

A dreadful silence fell over them. "A cover tune, eh?" Greg said. "What do you think, Jodie?"

"I—I don't do cover tunes," she said.

"You *do* know what a cover tune is?" Gary asked, with a smirk flirting around his lips.

"Well of course." She laughed helplessly.

"Well, if you don't want to sing any of the hits, and you don't know my stuff, it doesn't look like we can hear you tonight."

She deduced that a cover tune was a hit song from some famous record, and began to revise her decision on cover tunes. But as she looked around the room at the motley crew who would be listening, she found her nerve evaporating. They'd laugh and boo her off the stage—in front of Greg.

They were saved by the waiter, arriving with Gary's drink. Jodie decided it was time to start asking the questions she really wanted to ask and said, "Where are you from, Gary?"

"Sudbury."

"I'm from Waterloo. I have some friends here in Toronto. Have you run into the guys from SWAK? They're just new in town. I'd like to get in touch with them."

"SWAK? No, I never—hey, wait a minute. I met three guys at Steve's this afternoon. SWAK, yeah, that was it—young guys."

"Steve who?" she asked eagerly.

His surprised look told her she should know Steve. "Steve's Music Store—Queen at Bathurst. One of the guys was buying strings for his ax."

"Do you know where they're staying?"

"They didn't say, but I gave them guest passes for tonight. They might show. So, Greg, do you have ties with any of the big record companies?" Gary asked.

Greg knew it must be every struggling musician's dream to get signed with a known label. "I shop my groups around for the best deal. I'm not tied to any specific one," he replied.

"Any American labels?"

"Atlantic."

"Great! Look, I have to run, but let's get together later, Greg. Nice talking to you, Jodie."

Jodie and Greg exchanged a relieved look after he left. "I hope I didn't botch anything," Greg said apologetically.

"You did just fine—a lot better than I did. Whoever heard of a cover tune?"

"Musicians, I guess. I got worried when you were gone a while. Those guys looked pretty tough. How did it go backstage?"

"They didn't do anything, but let's just say I'm glad I didn't go to an audition alone. Do you think the boys will turn up? I don't think they'd waste guest passes."

"It may not even have been our boys he met. I think he just wanted to be agreeable, since I gave him the idea I might be helpful to him."

"It could have been them. He said young guys."

Greg thought that was vague enough to be meaningless. Jodie was young. Any group she knew would probably be around her own age. He didn't want to kill her hopes, and said, "What I'm wondering is what Bud was doing with an ax."

"It figures he wasn't chopping down trees in the middle of the city. If he was buying strings for it, he must have meant his guitar. More jargon. Since the boys might show up here, I suppose we should stay. I'll quiz Gary more closely about the guys he met at Steve's at the next intermission."

Greg gave a weary sigh. "That means more torture for the eardrums. I wish I'd brought earplugs."

"I have some paper tissues I plan to use." She tore strips off one and made ear plugs, which she put in her ears, although they weren't very effective.

It was a long night. The music and the crowd got louder and the beer less palatable as the evening progressed. The heavy, insistent beat of the music touched some primitive chord in the audience. It was an appeal to the sexual instinct, as blatant as a nude photograph, or the gyrating musicians on stage.

Greg's eyes moved to Jodie, and he noticed she was moving to the music, unconsciously exciting him. Greg wasn't immune to the rhythm, either, but he preferred more subtlety. The flashing lights were beginning to give him a headache. "Would it look strange if I put on my shades?" he asked, and put on his sunglasses to cut down the glare.

"Cool, Greg," she said, laughing.

Gradually the room had filled up. When Roar Shock stopped playing at midnight, there was a loud demand for an encore. They finished on their raucous theme song, "Sweet Kisses." Gary came to the mike and said, "Thank you, folks. We're gonna take five, but then we'll come back and play 'Sweet Kisses' for you, just one more time."

Greg and Jodie exchanged a helpless look. "I feel as if I'm trapped in *hell*," Jodie said.

"What do you say we leave?" Greg suggested. "I'll send a note backstage with my phone number."

Jodie really wanted to talk to Gary just to make sure it was Hank and the boys he'd seen at Steve's. She had an instinctive knowledge that Greg wouldn't like her going backstage again. She didn't look forward to it herself. She wouldn't go into their room, but just speak to Gary in the hall. "Why don't you go round up a cab and I'll write the note," she said.

Greg's quick tour around the room convinced him that no one would cause any trouble. People were no longer staring at them and appeared to be minding their own business now. It seemed safe to leave Jodie for two minutes. "Anything to speed our departure," he agreed, and left.

Jodie jotted down the hotel phone number then hurried toward the hall where the band's dressing room was located. The party had spilled out into the hallway. Gary and the other players were there, laughing and talking with some girls. When Gary saw her, he excused himself from the others and came toward her.

"Jonie." He smiled. He didn't remember her name.

"That's Jodie," she reminded him, handing him the note. "Greg and I have to leave now. This is the number where we can be reached. But before I go, I wanted to ask about SWAK—" His face didn't register recognition. "The group from Waterloo you saw at Steve's this afternoon."

"Oh yeah, SWAK. Right." The other people went into the room. Now they were alone in the dim hall. "What do you say we blow this joint and go up to my place?" he said.

"Greg's waiting for me. About SWAK, Gary." She described the three boys.

Gary listened, but with a glazed look in his eyes. "Sure sounds like them. The lead guitarist wanted me to try his Fender."

Bud didn't play a Fender guitar. He played a Gibson. And if she told Gary so, he'd just let on it had been a Gibson. She doubted he'd ever seen the boys, and if he had, he didn't remember. All she wanted at that moment was to escape without any trouble. "Thanks a lot, Gary. I have to go now."

He put his hand on her arm to detain her. That was all he was doing when Greg reached them, but Greg had seen that purple-haired drunkard leering at her, touching her, and a fury seized him. Already impatient from the long, torturous night, his temper broke. It was something visceral and primitive. Jodie saw the fire in his eyes and said, "I've got to go now, Gary." She grabbed Greg's hand and they fled. A crowd had collected at the doorway. Their mocking laughter followed the fleeing couple down the hall.

"You were supposed to send a note!" Greg growled.

"I delivered it in person to make sure he got it. Let's get out of here, fast!" Jodie said. They ran down the hall, out through the tavern where the impatient clients waited for the band's encore. The taxi was at the curb with the meter ticking. Greg helped Jodie in and got in beside her, too outraged to give their address.

"The Royal York," Jodie said.

"Why did you go back there?" Greg demanded.

"To give Gary the note."

"You were supposed to *send* the note."

"I changed my mind. It's a woman's prerogative."

"You have no more sense than a child. You should have foreseen what would happen."

"Nothing happened," she said, refusing to be intimidated by his anger, maintaining her composure.

"It would have, if I hadn't gone after you," he retorted.

"I can look after myself! I don't need you butting in."

As his anger passed, Greg was beginning to realize he had overreacted. Feeling as though he had made a fool of himself, he tried to change the subject. "Butting in is the man's prerogative. We've only been friends for a few hours, and we're already having our first fight."

"This is not a fight. It's a minor disagreement. Besides, you didn't ask me the important question."

Greg frowned in confusion. The important thing was that Jodie was all right. "He didn't have time to...hurt you."

"He had no intention of hurting me," she scoffed. "The important thing is finding the boys, and I don't think Gary saw them at all. He mentioned the lead guitar playing a Fender. Bud plays a Gibson."

"We've wasted a whole evening," he said, drawing in a weary sigh. "And to top it off, I spilled beer on my shirt."

"Is that what smells?" She opened the cab window. "In a way I'm glad Hank and the boys haven't had anything to do with Delaney."

He was studying Jodie now. Her face was just a pale, delicate image in the shadowed cab, but memory supplied the details: gold-flecked eyes, determined chin...beautiful. "Welcome back, Pollyanna."

"There's no point looking on the dark side. We'll find them," she said confidently. "The evening wasn't a complete waste. We've learned something about the business. Next time we'll know what a cover tune is. I should practice up a song, in case I get a real audition."

It no longer surprised him that Jodie would go to such lengths to find the boys. She was not only inventive and imaginative, she was also an extremely determined young lady. Her determination inspired him to match it. "I guess I should bone up on performers' contracts. It might come in handy."

She turned in surprise. "If SWAK gets an offer, you mean? I never thought—"

"I meant if Miss James gets an offer."

"Oh!" She laughed. "You were joking. That's why I misunderstood."

He was astonished. Good Lord, did she think he was that dull, that he never joked?

They reached the hotel. Once there, she went up to Greg's room to get her knapsack. Opening his suitcase, Greg took out a clean shirt. That afternoon, there had been a feeling of constraint between them. They had both been eager for privacy. Now neither of them gave it a second thought. Greg took off his shirt, then tossed it on the bed.

Jodie looked at his broad shoulders, not bothering to hide her interest. The masculine patch of hair on his chest stirred some instinctive response. His chest tapered in muscled ridges to a lean waist. He had the build of an athlete.

Greg read the frank admiration in her eyes. He became conscious of his nakedness then, and hastily put on his clean shirt. But he was flattered at her expression. For a moment, their eyes met, neither of them spoke, but the air prickled with electricity.

Jodie thought it was time to return to business, before anything more developed. She said, ''I wonder if the boys are working—maybe working nights. New employees usually get stuck with the worst shifts.''

Greg went along with this mundane conversation, but tension quivered beneath the surface, and they both knew it. ''Why would they take night jobs, when they'll eventually want to play nights?''

''The operative word there is eventually. In the meanwhile, they'll have to take whatever work they can get. Now, where would three unskilled laborers look for jobs? Restaurants, theaters...''

''I'll have Palmer check them out, and keep an eye on the music stores tomorrow, too.''

''And check out Queen Street again. They might be sleeping in the van for a few nights, until they find rooms. The vacancy rate is about 1% in Toronto.''

''In the van!'' Greg exclaimed. ''How would they shower? How could they sleep? We've got to find them and get them home. This is ridiculous! The music business is for lunatics.''

Jodie watched him closely. ''The rock music business, you mean. You wouldn't mind so much if Bud went to Juilliard, would you?''

''Right about now I mind his having anything to do with music. He'd be better off going to Harvard. Serious musicians have a rough row to hoe, too.''

''Bud's the one who'd have to do it. It's pretty rough doing a job you're not suited for.''

''The opportunity I'm offering would at least provide a stable life, with good income.''

Jodie didn't bother arguing any further. Greg was nice, but he had a blind spot where Bud was concerned. He wanted to live his life for his brother. She felt he did it out of concern for Bud, but that didn't make it right. Bud should be allowed to make his own decision. And when they found the boys, she'd encourage Bud to do it. But could he afford to go to Juilliard if Greg wouldn't help financially? His money was tied up in a trust fund, and naturally Greg would hold the reins.

"We'll just have to keep on looking till we find them," Greg said grimly.

"You mean now—tonight?" she asked. It had been a long day and an even longer night. Her head was throbbing and her feet ached from pounding the pavement.

Greg looked at her, suddenly feeling that what he had been thinking was selfish. If the boys were working nights, then he and Jodie should be searching at the likely places of employment at night. He'd tour the city after Jodie left. She appeared burned to the socket. There were purple smudges of fatigue under her eyes, and her face looked drawn. And in spite of it all, he wanted very much to take her in his arms and kiss her. The feeling had been growing all through that long night of listening to the primitive, stirring music in the club.

She reached up to adjust the straps at her neck. Her naked shoulders looked inviting. "You're not going to find them serving drinks in some bar, Greg," she said. She yawned, stretching luxuriously, like a cat in the sun. Greg didn't answer, because he was only half listening. "Hank and Gil are underage. They're probably washing dishes in some kitchen. You should get a good night's rest, and we'll continue in the morning."

He didn't want her to leave, but she had already vetoed the idea of staying at the hotel. "You're right. I'll drive you to your friend's apartment."

"I'll take a taxi."

"Let me drive you. I want to see you get inside your friend's door safely. And it'll give me one last chance to scour the streets before I go to bed."

Jodie didn't feel any resentment at his insistence. She knew he didn't really think she was helpless. He was just being protective, as he wanted to protect Bud. Too much of his protectiveness could be smothering, but a drive home was welcome.

"You might prove too much temptation for the taxi driver," he added lightly, taking her knapsack to carry it for her.

They went downstairs and Greg had his car brought around. The traffic had thinned, making driving easy. Jodie leaned her head back against the leather seat and watched the streetlights slide past. "We won't be hearing from Gary again. That lead has petered out."

"It never was a real lead."

After another block, she said, "I bet you didn't think you'd be celebrating your McMurchy deal in a crummy little bar. I don't think I thanked you for coming to my rescue."

He gave a rueful smile. "No, I wouldn't describe your reaction as thanks, exactly."

"Thanks. I did appreciate it."

"You're welcome. Incidentally, I celebrated the closing of the deal by having champagne with a very beautiful woman. And had a wonderful time, I might add."

"It was nice," she said dreamily. "You're not what I thought you'd be like at all."

"Dare I ask—what was that?"

A bemused smile flickered over her face. "Oh, all cut-and-dried, you know. The way you act at the office."

"The same way you act," he pointed out.

"I have to impress the boss. You don't. He sets the tone."

"There's something to be said for separating business and pleasure. We wouldn't get much work done if the female employees strolled around in jeans and T-shirts. Too distracting," he added, flashing her a smile. Jodie had a mental image of his secretary, Mrs. Coombs, a prim and proper middle-aged lady, in jeans, and laughed.

"You're picturing me in my tin chains and kerchief," Greg said.

What she was picturing was him without his shirt. "Egotist! I wasn't thinking of you at all," she said airily.

"I assume that when you fell into a fit of giggles, you were thinking of me. I'm crushed."

"That's the apartment building, on the right," she said, pointing to a high rise.

He pulled in and turned off the engine. If he was going to get a good-night kiss, this was the time. But he couldn't just attack her like a Gary Delaney, so he leaned back, hoping to work up to it gradually. "One o'clock," he said. "What time will I see you tomorrow? We could meet at the hotel for breakfast."

"I'll give you a buzz when I get up. Not late. About eight-thirty. I'm bushed." She picked up her knapsack and reached for the door.

"I'll go up with you," he said, and got out, frustrated. The moment had passed. He'd botched it.

He took her knapsack. "Got your key?" he asked.

Jodie riffled in her purse and found it. "What do you keep in there?" he asked. "It's nearly as big as your gunnysack."

"Just the essentials." She smiled, arranging the bag over her shoulder while they went to the door. "You know, brush, lipstick, tissues, wallet, food, keys, pen, a pad, a book in case I have a long wait somewhere, a toothbrush."

"A kitchen sink. What good is a toothbrush without water? I'll go up to the apartment with you," he said, and took the keys to unlock the door.

"Nobody's going to attack me on an elevator."

"You never know," he said with mock seriousness, and went to the elevator. "Some young ladies can attract undesirables the minute you turn your back."

The elevator was empty. "Now are you convinced?" she asked, looking all around the empty space.

"It might be stopped on the way up. When I take a lady out, I see her safely home."

The elevator reached the ninth floor without stopping. The hallway was perfectly vacant. "I'll make a run for it," she said. "You can wait here to see I'm not ambushed."

"I'll go with you. Who knows what may lurk within the apartment itself?"

"You're giving me the creeps, Greg!" she scolded. "Now I *am* afraid to go into the apartment alone. Nickie might not be back yet."

"Never fear, Super Greg is here," he said, taking her arm to accompany her down the hall.

Jodie unlocked the door. The apartment was in darkness. "Nickie! Anybody home?" she called. There was no answer. She felt for the light switch. As the apartment came into view, the cheerful, homey room dispelled her case of fright, and she said, "Now, are you satisfied, or do you insist on looking under the bed?"

"A good idea!"

"Go home, Greg, and quit feeling you have to protect the whole world." She was thinking of Bud, and Greg's unreasonable protectiveness in that direction. Between that and fatigue, she sounded querulous.

"Not the whole world. Just the people who matter to me," he said. He took her purse and tossed it on the sofa.

Silhouette's

Best Ever "Get Acquainted" Offer

Look what we'd give to hear from you

6 FREE GIFTS 6

Return This Sticker
and Get 6 Gifts—FREE
Compliments of Silhouette

▲ **GET ALL YOU ARE**
ENTITLED TO—AFFIX STICKER
TO RETURN CARD—MAIL TODAY ▲

This is our most fabulous offer ever...
AND THERE'S STILL ➤➤➤ MORE INSIDE.
Let's get acquainted.
Let's become friends—

Look what we've got for you:

... A FREE 20k gold electroplate chain
... plus a sampler set of 4 terrific Silhouette Romance™ novels, specially selected by our editors.

... PLUS a surprise mystery gift that will delight you.

All this just for trying our Reader Service!

If you wish to continue in the Reader Service, you'll get 6 new Silhouette Romance™ novels every month—before they're available in stores. That's SNEAK PREVIEWS for just $2.25* per book— and FREE home delivery besides!

Plus There's More!

With your monthly book shipments, you'll also get our newsletter, packed with news of your favorite authors and upcoming books—FREE! And as a valued reader, we'll be sending you additional free gifts from time to time— as a token of our appreciation for being a home subscriber.

THERE IS NO CATCH. You're not required to buy a single book, ever. You may cancel Reader Service privileges anytime, if you want. All you have to do is write "cancel" on your statement or simply return your shipment of books to us at our cost. The free gifts are yours anyway. It's a super-sweet deal if ever there was one. Try us and see!

Get 4 FREE full-length Silhouette Romance™ novels.

Plus

this lovely 20k gold electroplate chain

Plus

a surprise free gift

▼ PLUS LOTS MORE! MAIL THIS CARD TODAY ▼

Silhouette's Best-Ever "Get Acquainted" Offer

Yes, I'll try Silhouette books under the terms outlined on the opposite page. Send me 4 free Silhouette Romance™ novels, a free electroplated gold chain and a free mystery gift.

215 CIS HAYJ (U-S-R-03/90)

PLACE STICKER FOR 6 FREE GIFTS HERE

NAME _____

ADDRESS _____ APT. _____

CITY _____

STATE _____ ZIP CODE _____

PRINTED IN U.S.A.

Don't forget...

... Return this card today and receive 4 free books, free electroplated gold chain and free mystery gift.

... You will receive books before they're available in stores.

... No obligation to buy. You can cancel at any time by writing "cancel" on your statement or returning a shipment to us at our cost.

If offer card is missing, write to: Silhouette Books®
901 Fuhrmann Blvd., P.O. Box 1867, Buffalo, N.Y. 14269-1867

It was very heavy. "You should get a set of wheels for that," he said. "You're going to dislocate your shoulder."

"It's my shoulder! I'll dislocate it if I want to!"

"Touchy! I better let you go to bed. Your good humor is fading."

"Sorry," she said. "I didn't mean to snap at you. I guess it is fatigue." She realized she should calm down before bringing up the matter of Bud and Juilliard. That still had to be settled.

"That's all right. I want to see you in all your moods," he said, and gazed at her, with a small, anticipatory smile curving his lips. His eyes were glowing with emotion when his hands reached and went around her. He felt the brush of warm, satin flesh beneath his fingers, and a swell of excitement rose. Jodie looked at him with uncertainty. Her eyes were wide open, startled looking. "Jodie—" He pulled her into his arms and kissed her.

The unexpectedness of it caught her off guard. She was in his arms, being thoroughly kissed before she knew what was happening. It was the last thing she would have expected of Greg, but the ardor of his seizure told her there was pent-up passion being unleashed. He had been wanting to let himself go for a long time. Maybe longer than he realized.

His hands moved over her back in hungry, caressing strokes that prickled gently, like velvet, as he crushed her against him. When her soft breasts yielded to the firmness of his chest, she felt a shudder tremble through her. Greg felt it, too, and a soft moan issued from his throat as the pressure of his arms increased. The sound reverberated in the still apartment, exciting her. She felt triumphant, to have jarred Greg out of his usual calmness.

Echoes of the primitive, insistent rock beat pounded in her head. Behind her closed eyes, lights flashed in an unreal ecstasy of torment that seemed the right accompaniment to this moment. Greg—was it really Greg Edison kissing her as if he were losing all control? His tongue flickered against her lips in taunting, suggestive strokes that inflamed her imagination. Before she recovered from it, his tongue was inside her, exploring her mouth with masterly strokes, claiming his prize.

She should stop. What would he think of her? But at that moment, what did she care? One hand moved lower, fanning her hip, pulling her against him in a body hug from head to knee as the kiss became more demanding. It activated every nerve ending, and sent the hot blood throbbing to her head. Her breaths were stifled by his lips. She gasped and drew away.

His lips moved to her cheeks, nibbling moistly, finding the weakness of her ear to send a deluge of exquisite longing piercing through her. Her stomach muscles contracted in response to the onslaught. If he didn't stop... She withdrew and just looked at him, silently. His eyes were dark with passion, his face was lax. He was breathing heavily.

"God, Jodie. I'm sorry!" he said, surprised himself at what he had unleashed. "I only meant to kiss you goodnight." He held her hand, squeezing it so hard it hurt, but she welcomed the sensation. It distracted her from more troubling thoughts.

"Good night, Greg," she said. Her voice was a whisper. "It's all right. You just got carried away."

He swallowed convulsively. He was going to get carried away by those big green eyes again if he stayed here, but he hated to leave. At the top of her gown, he could see the incipient curve of her breasts, rising and falling as she breathed. He couldn't keep his eyes off them. They were full and tantalizing. "You're so beautiful," he said softly.

Seeing what drew his eyes, Jodie pulled away. "That's the oldest excuse in the book. You didn't see me attacking you when you took off your shirt."

"Maybe you weren't attracted," he said, smiling. Greg knew she was attracted all right. He hadn't been fooled by her response to his kiss. "You can feel free to contradict that. I won't fire you."

"No comment," she said discreetly.

"That's Miss James speaking. I think I prefer your other persona." He kissed her chastely on the cheek and left, smiling.

Greg took a circuitous route back to the hotel, scanning the streets as he drove, but his mind was half a mile away, back in the apartment, making passionate love with Jodie James.

Jodie heated a glass of milk before going to bed. She had another problem to wrestle with. Besides finding the boys from the band, and convincing Greg to let Bud go to Juilliard, how on earth was she ever going to work with Greg after this? Bad enough she had to live down the rest of this adventure, but how could she live down that kiss? How could he? She couldn't see any escape except quitting her job. The university had some job openings for programmers. Maybe she could get hired there. She'd rather take a cut in pay than have to go on working at Edison's.

Chapter Six

Jodie was sound asleep on the sofa when Nickie Sommers returned to her apartment that night. The girls didn't meet until breakfast the next morning. Nickie got up early and was dressed for work when Jodie woke up.

"Good morning. I've just made some coffee. Want a cup?" Nickie said.

"What time is it?" Jodie asked, sitting up and rubbing her eyes in confusion. The strange room fell into focus, and she remembered where she was. With realization came the memory of why she was there—Hank—and the old worry fell like a pall over her spirits. Then she remembered Greg, and a lazy, luxurious smile crept over her face.

"Seven-thirty, sleepyhead."

How was it possible for Nickie to look so good so early in the morning? Every sleek hair was in place. Not only was her short, black bob attractive, but her makeup was perfect, too. She could have posed for a professional business ad in her tailored dress with the white collar. Yet the brisk, businesslike air didn't detract from her femininity.

"Any luck in finding your brother?"

"Not really," Jodie replied, accepting the coffee. "Thanks."

"He'll turn up. It just takes a little time. Now, tell me all about the man you're with," Nickie demanded.

"It wasn't a date. He's my boss," Jodie explained. But the memory of how that evening had ended sent a warm flush of color to her cheeks.

"I see," Nickie said, with a knowing look. "It's a shame we don't have more time to talk while you're here, Jodie. Why don't we all get together for dinner tonight? You, your boss, and me. You can bring him here. I'll cook."

"No!" The response sounded so brusque that Jodie softened it with an excuse. "I can't make plans for him. I don't know yet what we'll be doing. We have a few things pending." She knew their tentative plan for dinner was to have lobster at the Mermaid, and didn't think Greg would mind if Nickie accompanied them. But she minded very much. Nickie was too darned pretty. Jodie consoled herself that it wasn't really a lie. Something might come up to change their plans, and why complicate it by involving a third party?

They talked while they had their coffee, and in a short while Nickie had to leave for work. The newspaper had been left at the door. Jodie took it to the table, then poured herself another cup of coffee. The paper was bulky, compared to the one at home. Of course Toronto was a lot bigger than Waterloo, with more things to report…and more places for Hank and the boys to disappear. It would take ages to find them by just looking at music stores and clubs. They could be anywhere. Queen Street wasn't the only area with cheap rents. There were dozens of suburban towns.

It would be a lucky fluke to find the boys in a shop. They would need guitar strings eventually, and Gil would need drumsticks maybe, but they might not need them for weeks. And neither she nor Greg could devote weeks to looking. Bud had often spoken of getting a demo tape made, but the boys might not be able to afford it for a month or more.

They'd turn up somewhere, sometime, but that wasn't good enough. Their families wanted them found now. Really, some small corner of her heart wasn't so keen to find Bud, and have him pressured into giving up his music. It wasn't fair. She was sure it was Greg's intransigence that had forced Bud to run away, and she half admired the boy for it. Being young, he had done it in a foolish way, involving his friends, but he had struck his blow for freedom. What right did she and Greg have to thwart his ambitions? Maybe none, but she had a duty to get Hank back, and she'd keep trying.

If she could just convince Greg, before they found Bud, to let him go to Juilliard, that would be the ideal solution. But how did you move an immovable object like Greg Edison, who thought he knew what was best for everybody? He had grown so accustomed to looking after Bud that he didn't realize his little brother had grown up.

Her eyes flickered over the paper. What would she do if she were looking for a job in Toronto? She'd read the Help Wanted columns. The boys, too, had probably started their search for work with the daily paper. There were pages of ads. She flipped past the professional positions, but that still left several pages of unskilled labor. It was pointless to think she could phone every number in the paper to make inquiries.

As her eye ran down the page, she felt a sense of depression seep into her bones. Dishwashers wanted, janitorial services, kitchen help... The music business was hard. If the boys didn't make it, and had no decent schooling behind them, they'd end up in dead-end jobs like these. She came to a dark line, and read the heading, Dramatic and Musical Talent. She hadn't realized that performing artists had their own special classified-ad column, although it made perfect sense once she thought about it.

Her heart beat more rapidly as she scanned the column. Bands!!!!! Secure Private Practice Space. She rooted a pen out of her purse and marked the ad. SWAK would need a place to practice. That would be one of the top priorities. Practicing in Waterloo had been a big problem. They'd resorted to renting space in a warehouse at the edge of town, where the noise wouldn't disturb the neighbors.

Most of the notices asked for one or two performers to complete a band. She didn't think the boys would be willing to break up, so she skipped over those, but the practice hall was a real possibility. She was eager to make the call that minute, but if she called too early, she'd probably get the receiver slammed in her ear. She ripped out the ad, then slid it in her purse to show Greg. Or would she?

Did she have the right to betray Bud? She could follow up this lead herself. It would be hard to get away from Greg to make the phone call during the morning. And if she learned anything helpful, like a phone number or address where the boys could be reached, then she'd have to give it some very serious thought. In the meantime she'd keep nagging at Greg to let Bud go to Juilliard.

It was time to get dressed and phone Greg. Eight-thirty, she'd told him. She felt a strong reluctance to put her costume back on. Nickie had looked so nice in her suit. It was the way she'd be dressing herself, if she were going to work today as she should be. Greg had seemed to like her much better last night when she was dressed in a more sophisticated manner. Instead, she'd have to impersonate a kid again.

She emptied the contents of her knapsack on the sofa and sorted through them. She chose the prettiest shirt there. It

was a simple white sleeveless jersey with some flowers em-
broidered around the neckline. It'd have to do. The day was
warm, and she piled her hair loosely on top of her head. She
laced a scarf through the loops of her jeans, leaving the ends
to dangle free.

She thought of Greg and his scarf as she tied the silky
knot, remembering his efforts to fit in by buying those cheap
chains. That had surprised her. Other things had surprised
her about him, too. He wasn't the stuffy kind of man she
had thought he was. He could be fun, and surprisingly sexy.
A twinge of guilt disturbed her thoughts. What would he say
if he knew she planned to work behind his back, to give Bud
a chance to escape? That was really what it amounted to.
She meant to get Hank and Gil back, but warn Bud to give
him time to move on. Greg would probably see it as a betrayal.

Well, too bad. Bud's life was his own. He had a lot of
musical talent; he deserved a chance to use it. It was a pity
that she had to go against Greg Edison to give Bud his
chance.

Before she called Greg, she folded the bedding from the
sofa and tidied up the kitchen. Greg's voice, cheerful and
alert, told her she hadn't got him out of bed.

"Have you had breakfast?" he asked.

"Just coffee."

"I was hoping you'd say that. I waited for you. Why
don't you grab a cab and meet me in the coffee shop here at
the hotel?"

There was more than friendship in his voice. It was warm
with eagerness to see her. Just then she was beginning to feel
like a traitor. "I'm just leaving."

"I'll save us a table."

"Okay. Bye."

She wouldn't be able to look him in the eye. She was a
terrible liar, and for the rest of this trip, she'd be acting out

a charade. Distracted by her thoughts, Jodie unthinkingly picked up her knapsack after she'd called the taxi. There was no reason to take it with her. She planned to return to Nickie's place to sleep again. Since they might find the boys today, however, she decided to take it along with her rather than go back upstairs and risk missing her taxi.

She was glad the sun was shining. It gave her an excuse to wear her sunglasses. Jodie left them on when she reached the hotel so Greg wouldn't see the betrayal in her eyes. There was a lineup at the coffee shop, but Greg had got them a seat and waved to her from the table. After the incident in the apartment the night before, she felt self-conscious, and unsure how to greet him.

Greg didn't have any such reservations. He noticed that she was carrying her knapsack, and wondered if she'd decided to stay at the hotel that night. He felt it was an acceptance of something—some trust at least between them.

He smiled and kissed her on the cheek. When he said, "Good morning," he looked at her in a special, intimate way that told her he hadn't forgotten last night, and didn't regret it. "Why the shades?" he asked.

"I'm just resting my eyes," she said evasively, picking up the menu.

A coffeepot and two cups were already on the table, and Greg was having coffee. He poured a cup for Jodie and said, "I've been eyeballing the breakfasts as they've been served. They do a tempting ham and eggs. Are you interested?"

She noticed his more relaxed conversation. He wouldn't have said *eyeballing* yesterday. "I usually just have orange juice and toast."

"You should have a better breakfast than that. Especially today, when we have a hard grind ahead of us. I recommend the ham and eggs."

Now he was worrying about her diet, and that suggested that he cared for her more than a little. "All right," she agreed, as she didn't want to bother arguing.

Greg cocked his head to one side and studied her. "You sound less than your usual enthusiastic self. Is something the matter?"

"I'm just a little depressed," she said, and drew a weary sigh.

He wanted to take her in his arms and reassure her that everything would be all right. He wanted to see her without her glasses, too. Perhaps by reading her eyes he could decipher whether or not she shared his growing interest. He hesitated to call it love, but he hadn't experienced anything like this strange euphoria before. It had come at a troublesome time, when he should be devoting all his attention to finding Bud.

"Drink your coffee. You'll feel better," he said gruffly because the atmosphere wasn't right for saying any of the things he wanted to say.

She sipped obediently. "Well, what do we do today? More of the same?" she asked.

A waitress came to take their order. As soon as she left Greg reached across the table and took her two hands in his. "Don't let it get you down, darling," he said. The *darling* surprised him as much as it surprised Jodie. He hadn't meant to say it, but his sympathy for her brought it out spontaneously. "We'll find them. It's just a matter of time. I've been scanning the papers, and I think I've got an idea."

She gave a jerk of alarm. The papers! He'd seen that ad too! "What do you mean?"

"I don't want to get your hopes up too high, but there's an ad here that might just draw our runaways." He handed the folded paper to her, pointing at a large ad. Her fingers trembled when she took the paper. It wasn't the page of ads she'd been reading, and her nerves settled down.

She had to remove her dark glasses to read, but at least she didn't have to look at him while she read. It was a half-page ad to Canada's Wonderland, a huge recreation park north of Toronto. It was similar to Disneyland, with a lake, restaurants, elaborate rides and various amusements. One feature was nightly concerts. The ad was for all kinds of musicians for summer work at a rate of pay that would seem exorbitant to the boys.

"But they want trained musicians," she pointed out.

"Bud's been taking lessons for years."

"Gil hasn't had any lessons at all."

"Drummers are often self-taught. Hank reads music, doesn't he?"

"Not as well as Bud. He taught himself from books. I doubt if he'd qualify for this."

"Well, Bud certainly would. I was talking to the waitress. She tells me all the high school kids who are in bands turn out for auditions. The boys might be there. It's a possibility anyway. I think we should check it out."

"Sure, why not? Where are they auditioning?"

"In the auditorium at Massey Hall, starting at ten." Greg was enjoying his breakfast, but he noticed that Jodie was just picking at her food. Seeing the troubled look in her eyes, he attributed it to worry about her brother.

"I wish you wouldn't let yourself get discouraged," he said bracingly. "It was unrealistic of us to think we'd get word of the boys so soon. It's a big city, but they'll turn up somewhere, sooner or later. We'll get a break. We just have to be patient. This might be the best thing that could have happened. It'll give Bud a taste of just how tough the music business is. I hope it puts some sense into his head."

Her reaction surprised him. "Maybe he's willing to suffer for something he believes in," she snapped, suddenly starting to eat her breakfast. Anger had finally lifted her from her depression. Let Greg waste his time hanging around at the auditions for trained musicians. If he thought his brother would forsake the band, he didn't know much about Bud.

She and Greg didn't both have to go. He could go alone. She'd make that phone call, and hopefully learn something she could follow up on.

"He doesn't know what he believes in," Greg countered. "He's too young to throw his life away. He's been seduced by the image of the rock star. He doesn't want to be a musician, he just wants to be a star, with girls throwing themselves at him. Did you see the number of girls in Delaney's room last night?"

"Your brother happens to take his music seriously, Greg. I don't think it's fair to compare him to Delaney," she snapped.

Annoyed by her unreasonable anger, he just tossed up his hands. "We'd all like to be rich and famous. That doesn't mean it's going to happen."

"It's like a lottery. You can't win if you don't play the game."

"And we know the odds of winning the lottery. About half as much chance as being struck by lightning—twice."

Jodie cut off another piece of ham and put it in her mouth, to prevent herself from saying some of the things she was feeling.

"Anyway," he said cajolingly, "there's no reason for us to argue about it. It's only Bud that I have anything to say about. If your brother and Gil want to continue with their music after they finish school, there's nothing to stop them—except common sense."

His condescending speech infuriated her. Banging their heads against a brick wall was fine for Gil and Hank, but it wouldn't do for an Edison. She steeled herself against guilt and pity and said, "I've been thinking, Greg. About that audition, there's no reason we should both go. I'll continue with the search while you check out Massey Hall."

"I thought we'd go together."

"Why waste time?"

"Levy and Palmer will be doing the usual tours."

"Three pairs of eyes are better than two."

"But—" But I want to be with you, was what he meant, and couldn't say. It was too selfish.

"Shall we meet back here for lunch?" she suggested blandly, and sipped her coffee.

"Fine." He studied her at length. Her eyes looked too large for her face, like a child's eyes, bright and luminous. Yet there was maturity in them, and strong determination in that delicate little chin.

When they finished breakfast, Greg said, "I should call the office, just to keep informed. I'll use the phone in my room."

"Good, then you can take my knapsack up with you," she said. It was hard to read his expression. His fixed smile implied confusion. "I brought it along in the hope that we'd find the boys today, then I could go home," she added stiffly.

"We'll meet here at twelve?" he asked.

"Okay."

"I'll get you the spare key from the desk, in case you get back earlier and want some place to rest. Feel free to use the phone, in spite of the inordinate cost," he added, still wearing that strange expression that was part smile, part something else. Memory, or anticipation.

"I just might do that."

Greg signed the bill and left, and Jodie sat on a moment alone, thinking. As soon as he left the hotel, she'd phone the practice hall. Would they give the information she wanted over the phone? Maybe she should ask Ron Almont to look into it for her. He'd offered to do anything he could to help. He might have come up with some new lead to follow, too.

She lingered at the doorway of the coffee shop till she saw Greg leave the hotel. He wore a frown of concentration. She wanted to run after him to apologize and explain. If her plan worked, he'd hate her. But if she didn't try, she'd hate herself. She had to go on living with herself. It wasn't likely she and Greg had any future, although his attitude suggested an interest in her at the present.

She felt too guilty to use his phone, and made her call from a pay phone in the lobby. "Ron, it's Jodie James," she said, and told him what she wanted.

"I'll be glad to look into it for you. A good thing you called me. I know most of the hall owners around town. They'll tell me the score. They're leery about giving out information over the phone, for security reasons. There's a lot of valuable equipment stored there. Where can I call you?"

"I'm just at the hotel temporarily. It'll be better if I call you again. How long do you think it'll take?"

"Give me thirty minutes."

"Thanks."

Half an hour wasn't long enough to do any serious looking, so Jodie just went back to the coffee shop and had another cup of coffee, which she didn't want. For thirty minutes she worried her conscience, but she didn't change her mind. She was doing the right thing.

Then she went and called Ron back from the pay phone again. "I think I've got what you're looking for," he said. Her spirits soared. "It's a practice hall out in an eastern suburb—Scarborough. I know the guy who owns it, Claude Wicke. He rents out six practice halls in a warehouse. One was taken yesterday. Three young fellows. A guy named Edison signed the lease. Is that your man?"

"Yes! He's the lead guitar. How can I ever thank you, Ron?"

"You'll owe me one. Here's the address. Got a pen?"

She rooted in her purse. "Shoot."

Jodie was exhilarated at her success, yet a shadow clouded what should have been pure joy. All they had to do was go out to Scarborough and wait. The boys practiced either during the day or at night. They might be there right now.... And if they were, Greg would clamp an arm on Bud and haul him back home.

So what should she do? Obviously she had to drive out to Scarborough herself to see if the boys were there. She'd try to convince Hank and Gil to go home, which left Bud in a bit of a bind. What would he do? It wasn't likely he'd stay on alone in Toronto. Now she'd have to do some prevaricating with Greg, to get away and rent a car that afternoon. She was almost sorry she'd got that lead on the boys.

Chapter Seven

Jodie checked the time and noticed it was only nine-thirty. It seemed much later. If she hurried, she'd have time to get out to Scarborough, find the boys and be back before lunch. A taxi would cost a fortune. She decided to rent a car. The easiest way to do it was through the hotel. By stressing the urgency, she got the company to have a car at the front door in half an hour. In the interval, she bought a map and studied the best route to Scarborough. At shortly after ten, she was on her way.

The city traffic was heavier than she was used to. Her carefully planned route went out the window after three blocks. The street she'd planned to take north was one-way south. She was soon lost, and had to keep driving till she could find a place to park and restudy the map. Eventually she was back on track, heading north.

The industrial part of Scarborough where the practice hall was situated was a maze of short streets, one-way streets and dead ends. She eventually found Wardain Road, only to discover that the buildings on it weren't numbered. It was a long line of warehouses painted in incongruous pastel colors. There was plenty of activity, but none of it suggested music.

Some truckers were unloading their rigs and others were loading crates into the back of their trucks. She drove slowly, looking for a street number or any evidence of musical activity. She first caught sight of Bud's blue van in the corner of her rearview mirror. She stopped with a jerk, looking over her shoulder. The van was parked at the side of a long yellow warehouse. She could hardly believe her luck. The boys must be there now!

Jodie slid her rented car in behind the van and started looking for a doorway into the building. A white Entrance sign lured her toward a door. As she approached it, a pair of German shepherds the size of ponies came lunging at her. The hair on their necks rose in warning. She ran back to her car with the dogs in pursuit, but they were on chains, and stopped a few yards beyond the warehouse door.

Now what? She had finally found where the boys were, yet she couldn't get to them. It was infuriating. There must be another door. She got out of the car again, and immediately the dogs set up a concert of barking. The racket was loud enough to bring a man out of the warehouse. He didn't look like a musician. He wore an ordinary blue sport shirt and trousers with a crease. His frown eased to a smile when he saw Jodie, cowering beside her car.

"Can I help you, Miss?" he asked.

"You can call off your dogs," she replied.

He patted them on their heads, and they subsided then to gentle growls of pleasure. "Gertie and Gilda won't hurt you. They're just our alarm system. I'm Stan Girard. What can I do for you?"

"I'm looking for a band called SWAK. This is their van, so I guess I've come to the right place."

"Oh yeah, the new kids on the block. They're in stalag five." He grinned. "Better put in your earplugs. They're rockers. I play jazz myself."

"That's nice. Will the dogs let me go in?"

"If they act up, I'll whup 'em," he said, as he escorted her in. A long corridor ran the length of the warehouse; it was punctuated with a series of numbered doors. The rooms were soundproofed, but the building shook with the music. When they reached number five, Jodie realized it was the source of the reverberations.

"Thanks," she said, and Stan left, rather reluctantly, to return to number one.

Jodie didn't know whether it was the music or her own nerves that made her hand tremble on the doorknob. Turning the knob slowly, she peered in. It was a familiar sight: the boys bent over their instruments, playing their hearts out. She'd been to a few rehearsals, and had even gone to their first school dance, to watch from the balcony. Gil's head bobbed and his arms moved in a blur of speed as he beat the drums. Bud and Hank reeled around the stage. The spontaneous choreography made their shows lively.

She listened a moment, feeling sorry she had to be the one to bring their dream to an end. They looked so carried away by the music. The music sounded pretty good, too, for amateurs. Of course ultimately they wouldn't be judged as amateurs. That's why they were practicing so hard. No one noticed her as she stood, listening. The hall wasn't air-conditioned. Perspiration glistened on the boys' faces, and rolled in rivulets down their foreheads. Bud wore a kerchief that he'd rolled into a sweatband around his head.

Suddenly the music dwindled out. Bud had stopped playing, and called the group together to talk. "Not tight enough, guys. You're half a beat behind, Gil. We're not playing reggae, you know. And Hank, you're missing that chord progression in the twelfth bar."

"I told you I couldn't do that," Hank objected. "Not when you play so fast. None of the other groups bother with chord progressions."

"We're not just any three-chord band," Bud reminded him. "We'll take it again from the top, and—"

Hank was first to spot Jodie. His mouth fell open. Bud saw him staring, and turned around. He uttered a short, explosive sound, just before his expression hardened to stone. In that split second, it was as if she were looking at Greg. The family resemblance was strong. She walked forward slowly, while they all stared at her, with varying degrees of dread.

"So you found us," Hank said, looking an apology at the others.

"The point is, what do you think you're going to do about it?" Bud asked. He assumed an arrogant attitude, one hand on his hip, feet splayed, but she could sense the uncertainty beneath the pose.

"We have to talk about that, guys," she said.

"You can talk all you want, we're not going back," Bud said firmly.

"Speak for yourself, Bud, but you don't speak for my brother," Jodie replied. "It's fine for you. You're eighteen, you're finished high school at least. If all else fails, you have a family business to fall back on. It was damned inconsiderate of you to haul these kids off before they even finished high school."

"It was our decision," Hank said. "We wanted to come."

"Yeah," Gil threw in, to show his solidarity.

"I didn't figure you came at gunpoint. Let's say Bud persuaded you. It was your idea, wasn't it, Bud?" She stared Bud in the eye, daring him to deny it. He didn't flinch, and that reminded her of Greg, too.

"Yeah, it was my idea. What about it? We're not asking anybody for permission, and we're not asking for help. We're going to make it on our own."

"We got jobs," Hank said.

"Where?"

"Mine's at Lennie's Pizzeria. All the free pizza I can eat." The childishness of Hank's answer only emphasized his youth.

Before Jodie could reply, Bud spoke again. "You can tell our families we're just fine, and we're not going home," he said. He turned away from her, as if the conversation were over.

"You can tell Greg yourself. He's in Toronto with me," Jodie replied.

The reaction was startling. First his body stiffened, then he wheeled around and stared at her as if she'd drawn a gun. His face was white and grim. He was afraid of Greg. Not physically afraid, but afraid he'd be convinced to give up his music. "Is he here?" Bud asked in a cold voice.

"Not right here. He's in Toronto, looking for you."

"Then he doesn't know you've found us?" Bud asked eagerly. Dropping his tough stance, he advanced, wearing the face of a child. "Don't rat on us, Jodie. This is our chance. Don't tell him." It was those dark eyes that made him seem like a young Greg, talking to her. Young and vulnerable.

"Can't *you* talk to him, Bud? Tell him how much your music means to you. You're of legal age. He can't *make* you go to Harvard. I believe you should go to Juilliard."

"He controls the money. Well, that's fair. He earned it. It's too expensive for me to put myself through Juilliard."

"You could work for a year or two, save your money." But she could see "a year or two" might as well be a lifetime to anyone as young and eager as Bud.

He just shook his head. "I'm staying. The guys are free to leave if they want," he said, looking at them.

Of course they wouldn't leave, even if they wanted to. They had to keep up a macho image within the group, and Jodie didn't think they wanted to leave yet anyway. "No way. We're a team. We're staying," Hank said. Gil nodded and murmured his agreement.

"Why did you run off in such a childish, underhanded way?" Jodie goaded. "That was really thoughtless of you. Since you're all so mature and able to handle things, you might have talked it over with your families. We've all been worried. Mom's nearly sick, Hank." The three exchanged a guilty look. Jodie knew bringing mothers into it was dirty pool, but she was determined.

"It was just to avoid hassles," Bud explained vaguely.

"You caused a lot of hassle for the rest of us. Greg and I have been here for two days, looking for you. The cops are looking for you, too. Greg's hired a private detective."

Bud put his hand on his head and groaned. "I might have known he'd do something stupid like that."

"I guess it runs in the family," Jodie said. "Why don't you talk to him, Bud?"

Bud shook his head. "You can't talk to Greg. His idea of talking is giving a lecture. Are you going to tell him you found us?" he asked.

She read the pleading on his young face, which was so much like Greg's. "You can't leave your brother just hanging, wondering what's happened to you. Greg has a right to know. He's worried about you, Bud."

"All he worries about is business—making money."

"Why do you think he does that?" she snapped back angrily. "To give you a better life than he had himself. You should be grateful."

"We didn't need such a big house for two of us. It's just to impress his clients."

"I don't think so."

"If he really cared, he'd let me to go Juilliard."

"If he agrees to that, will you see him? Will you and the guys go back home?"

"He won't agree to it," Bud said. "And even if he did, I couldn't abandon the guys. We're a team. We're going to make it together."

"Yeah," Gil said.

Jodie sensed Bud's interest. She was sure he'd change his mind if Greg would let him pursue his musical career in a more orderly fashion. And she knew that Bud was the instigator and mainspring of the whole band. That very fact, however, made it hard for him to back down. He'd led the boys on this merry chase. He must feel some responsibility. She'd have to work on Hank and Gil, as well as Bud.

When she spoke, she spoke to Gil and Hank. "You're young. Finish high school first, then pursue your goals."

"I don't see what difference one more year makes," Hank said.

"It makes the difference of a high school diploma—just in case you want to go on to college later," she pointed out.

"We can't leave. We've hired the hall. We've paid and everything," Hank said.

"It could be sublet. There's a shortage of practice halls."

"We were lucky to get this one, and we plan to continue using it," Bud said. "Is it unanimous, guys? We're all agreed we stay."

"Right!" Gil and Hank said, fairly firmly.

"So, are you going to tell Greg, or what?" Bud asked, trying to look unconcerned, but the pleading look was still there.

"Not right away. I'll talk to him, see if I can arrange a deal." Bud looked interested, and she continued. "But first *we* have to make a deal. If he agrees to Juilliard, will you give this up and come home?"

"No way!" he said promptly. "This band has made plans." He was as stubborn as his brother, but Jodie admitted that under different circumstances, she might call it determination, and admire it.

"But if he lets you go to Juilliard, Bud!" Hank said. "We wouldn't want to interfere with that. We know that's what you always wanted. Right, Gil?"

"Right, man."

"Maybe in the autumn..." Bud looked doubtfully at the boys. "We're staying for the summer at least. We've already got a gig lined up for a dance at Pearson High School. Summer school."

"Summer here *and* Juilliard—that'll be a tough sell," Jodie said.

"I'd have to stay for the summer to help the band get established," he explained. "By September I could find a new lead guitar, so I wouldn't be letting the guys down flat."

Jodie appreciated his scruples, but was sorry they were so troublesome. She doubted that the band meant as much to the others as it did to Bud, but if she said so, they'd deny it. They had temporarily convinced themselves the band was their whole life, and they were risking all for it. She remembered the romantic folly of youth.

"Andy Ross has always wanted to join us. He plays lead guitar," Gil mentioned. "He'll be back at school in September. What I mean is, SWAK could work the Waterloo high schools another year, so me and Hank could finish high school. Jodie's probably right about that."

She breathed a sigh of relief that Gil had come up with a compromise that might just work. They could all maintain their dignity, without ruining their lives. She noticed that Gil wasn't really upset at the prospect of Bud's leaving, and she thought Hank felt the same way. Already they were disenchanted with Bud's perfectionism. The big question was, could Greg be coerced into letting Bud stay in Toronto for the summer *and* attend music college?

She stayed for a while to find out where the boys were working, and where they were living. Gil worked with Hank in the pizza place on Queen Street. Bud, being eighteen, had taken a job as a waiter in a tavern. The pay wasn't much but the tips were good. They all worked from four till twelve, slept till eight and practiced most of the day. With the college students away for the summer, they'd found a sublet apartment near the practice hall, which explained why the van hadn't been spotted in Toronto. Paying the first and last month's rent had nearly cleaned them out.

"I better be going now," Jodie said. "I'll be in touch with you, then let you know if I have any luck with Greg."

"You won't tell him you found me?" Bud asked.

"I'll talk to you again before I tell him. I've got your phone number at work, and your address."

Hank walked her out to the car, because of the dogs. As soon as they were out of the room, he said, "How did Mom take it?"

"How do you think? She's really worried, Hank."

"You'll tell her I'm okay."

The big dogs came up to Hank, and he began stroking them, running his hand from the crown of their heads down their necks and shoulders. They gave whining sounds of ecstasy. "Nice sleek coat, but these poor dogs should be exercised. I wonder if Claude would mind if I walked them."

Jodie didn't venture an opinion, but she noticed that Hank didn't look nearly as happy playing his bass as he looked right now, surrounded by animals. "How's Duke?" he asked.

"Lonesome. He whined like a baby the night you left."

"I wish I could have brought him with me."

"What about your veterinarian's course, Hank? Didn't you mind giving that up?"

He looked as troubled as Jodie felt. "Yeah, but Bud really is good, you know. He might have made a success of SWAK. That would have been neat. If you do make it, you only have to work a few years and you're rich for life. Eventually I planned to do something else. If Bud leaves the group, me and Gil will keep it up for fun next year at school, the way it was in the first place."

After graduation he'd go to veterinarian college. He didn't have to say it, but his smile when he petted the dogs said it all. Animals were Hank's life. This summer spree was just to get the music bug out of his system, and provide some excitement. It was practically a tradition for young men to run away once, to try their fledgling wings. Who didn't harbor that universal dream of making a million? She hoped the boys could have their summer fling, but when she thought of Greg Edison's determination, she wasn't at all sure of it.

"I'd better get back to the hotel," she said. "I'm meeting Greg there."

"Where is he anyway?"

"At the Wonderland auditions at Massey Hall. They're trying out musicians there today. He thought Bud might try out. The pay's very good."

"How did you find us?" he asked. Jodie told him briefly of the search.

When she left, Hank gave her a shy hug. "Look after Mom and Duke for me, Jodie."

"I will. In that order."

"Sorry I was such a bother."

"I forgive you this time, Hank. Take care of yourself."

She left. If she didn't hit a traffic jam, she figured she should just make it to the hotel by noon. Traffic was heavier as noon approached, however, and by the time she left the car at the hotel door to be picked up, it was twelve-fifteen. She hurried into the lobby, wondering how she could account to Greg for her morning. She'd say she'd been looking for the boys. That was true. She didn't have to tell him she'd found them.

In the lobby, she stopped, trying to remember where she was supposed to meet him. Was it the coffee shop, or his room? She was flustered from hurrying, worried because of the deception she was involved in, yet she was eager to see Greg.

Greg had been waiting since noon. He spotted her first and when he saw her, his worried frown eased to a smile. It had been a long, frustrating, profitless morning at Massey Hall. He had left there in a black temper, but one sight of Jodie and his spirits lifted. She was taking this whole affair very hard. She looked frazzled, poor girl. Frazzled but still totally adorable. He decided he liked her better in the un-businesslike outfits she'd been wearing in Toronto. She had turned from a competent employee into a spontaneous, unpredictable woman right before his eyes.

He hurried toward her and took her arm. He wanted to touch her, to feel the reassuring solidity of her. When they were apart, he sometimes feared he'd imagined her. "You need a cold drink and some lunch," he said. "Where do you want to eat?"

"Can we eat here in the hotel?"

"The main dining room isn't open for lunch."

"I didn't mean the Imperial Room. The coffee shop's fine."

Greg wanted something better than a booth and an Arborite table, suggesting instead that they lunch in the hotel's Black Knight dining room. It was dimly lighted, providing a more intimate atmosphere. Jodie appreciated the ambience. She didn't want Greg to be able to see her too clearly when she did her prevaricating.

"What did you do all morning?" he asked, as soon as they were seated.

"I went down to the radio station to see if they had any ideas," she said. "I looked around town—you know. How about you?" she asked hastily, to change the subject from her search. "Did you learn anything at Massey Hall?"

"The boys weren't there, but every other young musician in town must have been. I'm sure they'll turn up there sooner or later. I think we should go back this afternoon."

Jodie would have hours to persuade Greg to do what Bud and she wanted. "We might as well," she agreed.

The waiter came to take their order. Jodie ordered the fruit plate with cottage cheese. Greg asked for the Caesar salad and cold cuts. "A beer would hit the spot while we wait," he added. Jodie had one, too, and they drank and talked till lunch arrived.

"You talked to the office before you left?" she asked.

"Yes. It seems I'm not as necessary there as I like to think. Everything's going on fine without me."

"Maybe you've been working too hard, Greg. I mean—" She meant he should have spent more time with Bud. Talked to him.

"I try to keep on top of things. It's the boss's job. When Bud's a little older, I'll be able to delegate some of the responsibility to him. Responsibility is good for young men. It teaches them leadership qualities." He gave her a flashing grin. "Look at the sterling character it made of me."

"Actually, Bud has leadership qualities. This escapade was his idea."

"I see his behavior as irresponsible. Dad was the disciplinarian in the family when I was a kid." Jodie wondered if that was where he'd got his idea that authority figures had to be tough. "Now it's my turn," he continued. "I suppose Bud sees me as the enemy."

"If you're trying to prevent him from doing what he wants with his life, you *are* his enemy."

He gave her a quick, startled look. "What I said is, Bud sees me as an enemy. I certainly don't see myself in that light. I want what's best for him."

"You want what you think is best for him. Doesn't Bud have anything to say about it?"

"If he has, he didn't say it to me. He just picked up and left. No explanation. He just ran away, which was capricious, careless."

"I think sometimes that's all a young person can do, Greg," she said, in a calm, reasonable way. "Sometimes the parents, or in Bud's case the older brother, don't really listen. He wants to be a musician, and I expect he will be, whether you like it or not. I don't see why you can't accept that."

"Accept my brother dressing up like a clown, wasting his life in noisy bars playing that god-awful rock! If it were decent music . . ."

"But he wants to play decent music. This band is just his ticket out of Harvard."

"You seem to know an awful lot about him."

"He was at the house a lot," she said evasively.

Greg sat a minute, thinking. "If he came home, we could discuss it rationally. I don't see how I could reasonably refuse to let him go to Juilliard. It's a prestigious college, and Bud has undoubtedly got musical talent. I wouldn't have refused, if only he'd discussed it with me."

Jodie stared, unable to believe her ears. "You would have let him go!" When the fact had truly sunk in, she felt light with relief and joy.

"I admit I'd prefer Harvard, but with a first-rate musical education behind him, Bud would certainly be able to make a good living. Either composing, or arranging, or playing the piano. I'm sure he'd do very well for himself."

"You might have told him so!" she said. "Didn't you two ever *talk*?"

"I tried! I would have told him so, if he'd ever asked me. I'd be perfectly willing to let him go to the college of his choice, if he'd agree to come home now. But before we can iron that out, we have to find him."

Jodie's soaring spirits sank a little. "If he'd agree to come home now..." That was exactly what Bud wouldn't do. He was as stubborn as his brother, and he had to protect his image with the boys. She still had some convincing to do before she told Greg she'd found the boys. Somebody would just have to do a little compromising.

"You know boys that age," she said, trying to sound him out. "Their egos are involved. It'd be hard to back out now. He'd feel he was letting the band down."

"The whole band will be coming home. Or am I wrong in thinking you want your brother back, too? Isn't that why we're here?"

"I want Hank back. But I'm beginning to think one summer here won't do them any harm, as long as they're back for school in September. Most boys run away once in their lives. Didn't you ever want to run away?" Maybe if she could bring back the memories of his youth, he might see things differently.

"I didn't have that choice. My father was ill. I wasn't much older than Bud when I became my brother's legal guardian, and had to behave like an adult. I guess it makes you grow up fast. Bud has some growing up to do, and he won't do it here, with no one to advise him. When we find him, I'll take him home," he said firmly.

Jodie listened carefully. "*If* you find him," she said. "My dad died when I was about that age, too. I didn't have to suddenly become the head of the family, but I had to stop being a kid to help Mom. It does—change a person," she admitted. She wished she had known Greg before his father died. He must have been more easygoing and relaxed then.

When their lunch arrived, they stopped talking about the boys. "I'm looking forward to our seafood dinner this evening," he said. "It's all that kept me from having a nervous breakdown this morning, while I sat for hours, listening to loud, atonal music."

She saw the gleam of anticipation in his eyes, and knew there was an answering one in hers, because in spite of that authoritarian streak in him, she found Greg could be very easy to love. "I'm looking forward to it, too."

"Do you really have to stay with your friend Nickie tonight?" Her eyes widened in alarm. What was he suggesting? "I just thought we might have a few moments alone, if you took a room here. It'd be more convenient for the morning, too. I'm not suggesting we share a room."

"I hope not! I'm already dreading having to work for you when all this is over."

"And here I've been looking forward to it with pleasure. I had no idea you were so—special," he said, hesitating over the word. He wasn't happy with it. "You never complain. You're good natured, intelligent—beautiful." He smiled softly when he saw the blush shade her neckline and travel up to her cheeks.

He wouldn't be saying these things if he knew what she was doing. "I'm not anything special," she said in a small voice.

"Modest, too! You're hogging all the virtues—except leadership."

And veracity! How could she go on lying to him? "If you want to honor me with a virtue, I suggest compassion. I can see the boys' point of view. I wouldn't want to ruin their plans, without leaving them something. I mean—well, what's the harm if they stayed here for the summer, Greg?"

"That's your youth talking," he said in an avuncular way. "When you're a little older, you'll realize that all those tired old clichés are true. 'As the twig bends, so grows the bough.'

A summer might be enough to get them in trouble. Give them a taste for the footloose life.''

"Two or three months aren't enough to change a person's character.''

"I feel two days have begun to change the way I feel.'' His eyes caressed her, and she knew he was talking about his feelings for her. Every moment they were together it became harder to deceive him. She understood why Greg was a little stiff and authoritarian. How could he be any other way, when he had had to grow up too soon, too fast? She felt in her bones she could help him loosen up and learn how to relax, with time. She already found him charming, and his charm was distracting her when she should be trying to convince him he was wrong.

"Aren't you contradicting yourself?'' she asked, frowning. "As the twig bends—but in two days it changes direction.''

"Either you weren't listening, or I didn't make myself clear. As you're usually a sharp listener, it seems the fault is mine. The twig is character. Feelings are something else.'' His dark eyes studied her. "It's my feelings that are changing. I've never felt this—''

As much as she wanted to hear it, she couldn't let him say it. She felt too guilty. "Oh, I'm sure you made yourself clear,'' she blurted out. "I probably just wasn't listening. It's hard to think, with all this hanging over our heads.''

She noticed that Greg was surprised at her sudden interruption at that particular moment. What would he think when he discovered the truth, that the woman he was gazing at as if he loved her was scheming behind his back to sabotage him? Jodie's lovely fresh fruit suddenly tasted sour.

"I guess it can wait,'' he said.

"I can't eat any more. Since you're finished, we might as well go on to Massey Hall. It's one o'clock.''

Chapter Eight

Jodie was sure that if she couldn't convince Greg to let Bud have his summer in Toronto, she could convince Bud to give it up. Surely his being allowed to go to music college was the important thing. There was really very little point in the band staying here a few months, if they were only going to break up in the autumn. It was just a young man's need to show himself a man of principle that stood in the way. Yet it seemed hard to try to dissuade a person from exercising his principles.

She had to see Bud, or talk to him. The practice hall didn't have a phone. Until he showed up for work at four, there was nothing more she could so, so she went with Greg to Massey Hall.

The place was swarming with musicians of all ages and both sexes, from gray-haired women in hats to ten- and twelve-year-old kids, but mostly teenagers. It seemed the whole world wanted to be part of show biz.

"It won't be easy spotting the boys here," Jodie said, as they were pulled along in the surging crowd.

"I've already checked SWAK hasn't arranged an audition. I did that this morning. Some people had the foresight to make appointments. If the boys come, they'll have to sign up at that desk," Greg said, pointing to a freestanding desk in the hall, positioned to catch incoming traffic.

"If they have to stop at the desk, then we can get out of this lineup and watch the desk from a distance."

Greg's greater height let him scan the room over the tops of other heads. "There are some chairs along that wall," he told her, pointing to the left. "Hang on. I'll try to mow a way through." He clasped her hand, then formed a driving wedge through the crowd. They reached the chairs and sat down to wait.

The whole hall was filling up with people waiting for their auditions. Excited groups were talking, some of them practicing their singing a cappella. Barbershop quartets sang in harmony. One man was playing a mouth organ, another was tuning up his fiddle, and in the corner, a pair of young men were tap-dancing. It was like a musical tower of Babel, with no one paying the least attention to anyone else.

"It's incredible how many people want to be performers," Greg said, shaking his head in disbelief.

"Our brothers aren't any different from the rest of the world," she answered. "You said you couldn't understand why Bud had done this—left home. Now you know. Everybody wants to be in show biz. It's just human nature. It might be a good idea for them to get it out of their system this summer." She hoped that repetition might make the idea more acceptable.

"We've already had this discussion, haven't we?" he asked. "Are you rehearsing to leave me alone in my search?"

"No! Why do you think that?"

"Why else have you suddenly said—twice—that you
think we should let the boys stay here?" She couldn't think
of any answer on the spur of the moment. "There's really
no reason you must stay," Greg continued. "I can carry on
alone a few days, if there's some reason you want to get
home. You've already done more than anyone could expect.
I'm perfectly aware that this mess is Bud's fault. As you
said, he's the oldest, and the leader of the band. But I hope
you'll stay with me. It makes the job more—interesting."

Jodie was gratified by his praise. When he looked at her
like that, she couldn't bear the thought of going. "I don't
want to leave!"

"Good." He took her hand and smiled intimately. "Neither do I. I'm beginning to think Bud's running away was a
good idea."

Her first little gasp of pleasure was for Bud's sake. She
thought Greg was having second thoughts, but that lingering smile told her his reason was more personal. He meant
he was happy because it had brought them together. A warm
glow spread like sunshine through her, and reflected in her
face. "I'm glad too." Then she remembered her plan of
repetition and said, "After all, no real harm's been done."

"I wasn't referring to our miscreants."

"I know."

He didn't say anything more, and neither did Jodie, but
there was a feeling of intimacy in just sitting there with him,
holding hands. It didn't matter much where you were when
you were falling in love, as long as you were with that special
person. Love created its own private oasis, insulating them
from reality for a moment.

"Did your brother always want to be a musician, or is this
a fairly new obsession?" he said, as they settled in to wait.

She was gratified to see he was finally taking an interest
in someone other than Bud. She talked about Hank and his
love of animals.

"How about Gil Turner?" he asked.

"Gil was always kind of reclusive. It's hard to know what he might have had in mind, but I know he loves his computer. He talks to me about that once in a while. I'm sure he'd do well in computer science."

As they talked, the crowd kept coming, swelling and filling the hall. The noisy space became muggy and the hard chairs offered little comfort. Greg leaned over and said, "We can see the people coming in just as well from outside. Shall we go out for a breath of air?"

Jodie got up eagerly. "I was just going to suggest it. My feet are falling asleep."

"Lucky feet! They don't have to listen to all the caterwauling in here."

They went out, hand in hand, into the sunlight. "Let's check out the parking lot," Jodie suggested. "The van would be easier to spot than the boys."

"They'd probably take a bus or subway to avoid the parking jungle. The Eaton Centre garage is the closest place."

"Maybe they're not as smart as you," she joked, and they walked along, peering across the road into the garage.

An acre of roofs gleamed in the sunlight. Short of patrolling the lot, there was no way of knowing if a blue wreck was there.

"Well, it was an idea," she said. "We'll go back and watch the door."

They returned to the front of the building. Jodie had plenty of latent worries, but at that particular moment, she couldn't see any imminent danger. The only shadow looming over her pleasant moments with Greg, was guilt for her deception. She wanted to share her discovery with him. But in fairness to Bud, she'd do as she had promised.

She still had a few hours to change Greg's mind. At dinner that evening, she'd make one last effort. If she failed to convince him to let Bud stay here for the summer, then she'd reveal Bud's whereabouts and let them fight it out. The important thing was that Bud go to Juilliard. If worse came to worst, he'd just have to compromise a little, especially as Hank and Gil didn't really mind.

They walked toward a stand of ornamental trees that gave some shade, while still allowing them to see the new arrivals. It was peaceful there, a little removed from the crowd. There were even birds in the trees, and a squirrel scurrying around a small patch of grass. "What we should have brought is a hammock," Greg said, eyeing the cool shade between the trees.

"Yes, it sure—" Jodie felt the words choke in her throat. It was impossible! What was Bud Edison doing here? He had obviously just got off the bus that was already moving down the street. He should be at the practice hall, or getting ready for work. It was as if she were seeing a mirage. On a second look, there was no mistaking Bud's tall, lanky frame, the same general shape as his brother's, but not so well filled out yet. He had changed his clothes from that morning. He now wore a plain blue T-shirt and jeans, with his hair neatly brushed. He was carrying his guitar case.

Jodie looked to see if the others were with him. He was alone. What could it mean? She had told Hank that Greg had been here this morning. Maybe Bud had come looking for him! Her eyes turned frantically from Bud to Greg. Greg hadn't seen him yet, but he was looking at her strangely.

"What's the matter?" he asked. "Did you spot Bud's van?" He glanced out at the road, where cars whizzed past. She didn't answer but just gulped, and looked back at Bud. Greg followed the line of her gaze. He came to rigid attention, shouted "It's him!" and shot forward to intercept his brother.

Jodie knew then that Bud hadn't come looking for his brother. He turned on his heel and started to run, but not before Greg had seen the frightened look on his face. The throng of people made escape impossible. Bud was blocked and slowed down at every effort. Greg soon caught him and put a strong hand on his shoulder. Bud turned slowly. Jodie watched with a sinking heart as the brothers glared at each other. "You don't run off this time, Bud. You have a little explaining to do!" Greg said angrily.

Bud was breathing hard, but he tried to act with bravado. He gave his brother a dismissing look and spoke to Jodie. "So you told him! Thanks a lot for setting me up, Jodie. I thought you were my friend. You promised to help me."

Her instinctive reaction was to defend herself, without thinking how it would sound to Greg. "I didn't tell him! I had no idea you'd come here. What are you doing here anyway?"

"Following your advice. You told Hank the pay was great. I'm trying to get up an audition for SWAK."

Greg stood, listening in confusion, trying to make sense of what they were saying. It sounded as if Jodie had been talking to the boys, as if she knew where they were all along—as if she'd been helping them. "You promised to help me," Bud said. But that was impossible; she'd been helping him find Bud and the others.

"That's not why I told Hank," Jodie protested. "I just happened to mention it. I didn't set you up, Bud."

"I suppose Greg isn't paying you to spy on us, either."

She felt a pronounced urge to slap his angry young face. "I don't have to be paid to look after my own kid brother. My only interest in all this is that you talked Hank into running away from home with you."

Greg's instinctive response was to defend Jodie when Bud verbally attacked her, even though she had betrayed him. He also felt a contradictory urge to defend Bud. His anger and frustration were spreading unevenly over them both.

"Miss James works for me as an office employee only," he informed his brother. Then he gave her a sneering look of dark accusation. "I can assure you she didn't tell me she'd been talking to you. On the contrary, she's gone to a lot of trouble to keep me from finding you. I've succeeded in spite of her."

"Greg, I wasn't—" He turned his head away, as if he couldn't stand the sight of her. Jodie stopped in mid-speech. What was the point? Nobody believed her. She had become an enemy to both the men she was trying to help.

"You're coming home with me, Bud. Where's your van?" Greg barked.

Bud took a deep breath and stood his ground. "I'm not going home, Greg. I'm not a little kid you can lead around by the nose any longer. I'm staying here, so you might as well go back home and start grooming some other robot for the corporate life." He leveled a cool glare at the hand holding his shoulder.

It seemed to Greg that in the two days since Bud had left home, he had turned into a man. He felt he was confronting a man now, not a kid, but the old habits of behavior were hard to change. "Don't be such a damned idiot!" he scoffed.

Bud's face darkened. "Anybody that doesn't do what you want them to do is an idiot, eh, Greg? Well, I got news for you. You don't know everything. You just think you do. In fact, you're the idiot. There's more to life than balance sheets and contracts and mergers. You live in a world of numbers and papers. I want to live in the real world."

"Yes, the world of drugs and slummy bars and groupies. You're an Edison."

"Spare me. I'm trying to forget it," Bud growled.

Greg just looked at him, bewildered. Bud had never spoken to him like this before. He had always been apologetic, or pleading—sometimes flaring into little bursts of anger, but never this cold, implacable manner that seemed like hatred. Bud saw the anguished incomprehension on his brother's face and added less angrily, "Don't try to stop me, Greg. It's *my* life."

Greg's hand turned lax and fell from Bud's shoulder. "But why?" he asked.

"You wouldn't understand. It doesn't have anything to do with money." On that speech, more wounding because it wasn't even meant to offend, Bud turned and left. He just walked away, while his brother watched him go in frustration. You couldn't grapple a grown man to the ground and browbeat him. He'd lost Bud. Not only the physical company of a younger brother, he'd lost his love and respect. He had failed. For a moment he was too overcome to speak.

Jodie saw him suffering, and hurt for him. She put her hand gently on his arm. "He'll get over it, Greg. He didn't mean it," she said softly.

His voice, when he finally spoke, fell like snowflakes, softly, icily. He was beyond simple anger, and spoke with a curious detachment. "You would know, of course. You've been in his confidence all along."

"That's not true."

"You told him about the auditions here. You didn't know about them until I told you this morning." His voice was flat, because he didn't dare give way to emotion.

"I only found the boys this morning."

"So that's why you were so eager to get away from me. How did you do it?"

"I got a lead on where they practice."

"Odd you didn't mention it at lunch."

"Greg, I can explain—"

He had already turned away from her, but before he did, he gave her a look that would keep her awake nights. It wasn't the angry glare she expected. It wasn't even accusing. It was disillusioned, sorrowful. It was the look of a man whose love had just turned to indifference. He stopped and turned back. "What good are explanations, when I can't believe a word you say?" Then, like Bud, he too walked away, leaving Jodie alone. Even standing in the brilliant sunshine, she felt empty and cold inside.

She saw the red bus coming down the road. Greg was in the crowd that got aboard. She had no idea where Bud had gone. After the bus left, Jodie wandered to the corner and waited for the next one. She didn't know where to go, or even why she got on the bus, except that she knew she was going to cry, and she didn't want to do it in front of so many people. The bus was headed downtown. Wanting to avoid going back to the hotel, she decided to go to Nickie's.

She got off at the next stop and hailed a cab to Nick's apartment. It was a good thing she'd kept her key. The apartment was quiet and lonely. The only sound was the hum of the air conditioner. Jodie slumped onto the sofa and cradled her big purse in her lap, because she needed something to hold on to. She felt if she let go of it, she'd fly apart. The weight of the world seemed to be pressing on her shoulders, but surprisingly, tears didn't come. She was too sad for tears.

She'd made a colossal mess of things. She should have told Greg she'd found the boys when she met him for lunch. But she'd promised Bud.... That was her mistake. She shouldn't have made that rash promise. If only she hadn't mentioned the auditions at Massey Hall to Hank....

What evil genie had made Bud go there? Recriminations were futile. She couldn't turn back the clock; what was done was done. Each act seemed right at the time. What was wrong with trying to help Bud and Greg work their problem out? That was all she was doing, trying to help. And her thanks was to be insulted by both of them.

Her sorrow congealed to anger. She was through with serving as mediator for the Edisons. Let them handle their own problem. Her only real concern was Hank. She lifted the receiver and phoned the Royal York. Greg answered his phone on the first ring. She had a vivid picture of him, sitting alone in that room, worrying about Bud.

"It's Miss James," she said. "I thought you might like to know where Bud's working, in case you want to talk to him before you leave town."

"Yes." How could a monosyllable sound so insulting?

"It's Mike's Tavern, on Dalhousie between Queen and Dundas streets. He goes on duty at four."

"Do you know where he's staying?" She read in his grim tones his opinion of an Edison serving beer. It was even lower than slinging hash.

"In an apartment in Scarborough, near the practice hall they hired." She gave the address of the hall and the apartment house. She realized perfectly well that he was wondering how she knew all this, and putting the worst possible construction on it. He'd probably leap to the conclusion that she had helped them find rooms, and planned their entire escapade.

"I'll notify Levy and Palmer to call off the search. Where are you calling from?"

Jodie felt a surge of hope. Was he going to come? "I'm at Nickie's place."

"You left your bag here. Shall I send it on to Nickie's apartment? I could put it in a cab. . . ."

This was his indirect way of saying he didn't want to see her again. The seafood dinner was cancelled. He wasn't the only one who could show how he felt about meeting again. "Why don't you just ask the hotel to check it? I'll pick it up when I go to the station to catch the train home," she said coolly.

"You're taking the train home then?"

"Yes." There was a longish silence. Jodie hoped he'd object, that he'd say that wasn't necessary, since he was driving home.

"Very well. I'll be calling on Bud. I want to see him before he gets to work, if possible."

"That might be best. He'd probably be too busy to talk at work, but I doubt if he'd have time to go back to the apartment."

"Is that where you meet him, at his apartment?"

Meet, not *met*, as though she'd seen him a dozen times. She didn't even bother defending herself. "No, I spoke to him at the practice hall. You could wait outside where he works."

"Do you have any message for your brother?"

"I know where he works. I can talk to him myself before I leave. I just thought you might want to know where you can get in touch with Bud—to apologize," she added, in a fit of pique. She fully expected to hear an explosion from the phone receiver.

"Thanks for calling."

"You're welcome. Goodbye, Mr. Edison." She replaced the receiver and clamped her lips shut tightly, to keep them from wobbling. She wanted very much to cry. He hated her. He could have offered to bring her bag over himself if he really wanted to see her. He could at least have scolded her, and given them both a chance to blow off some steam. But no, he didn't believe in displaying emotions. Bud was right. He was a robot.

But he hadn't been like a robot last night. He had been warm and loving. He certainly didn't kiss like a robot. Jodie fell into a daydreaming state. How good it had felt to be held in his arms. Having lost track of time, she looked at her watch. Three-thirty. She wanted to see Hank before she left for home. There wasn't time to go to his room, but she'd drop by Lennie's Pizzeria and talk to him there. It seemed

that since Bud had stuck to his guns, the group would be
staying in Toronto, not only for the summer, but maybe in-
definitely. And Bud wouldn't be going to Juilliard after all.
Such a shame... It didn't seem right that Greg's intransigence and stubbornness should keep his brother from doing
what he wanted to do.

She made a cup of tea to calm her nerves and sat alone in
the still apartment, thinking. She should have told Bud that
Greg had no objection to Juilliard. He had a right to know.
Maybe that was why Greg wanted to see him. It would be
good if she had some firm news to take home to her mom
and Mrs. Turner. At least she knew where the boys were,
and that they weren't starving or suffering.

Jodie thought of phoning her mother, but put it off. She'd
be going home that night. Might as well wait till she'd spoken to Hank. She called the station and got the schedule. A
train would be leaving at 8:30 p.m. She'd talk to Hank at the
pizzeria, maybe have dinner there, as an excuse to linger,
then catch the train home. Finding a piece of notepaper in
the kitchen, Jodie wrote a thank-you note to Nickie, which
she left on the counter, with the apartment key on top.

At four o'clock she went to the bathroom and looked
disconsolately into the mirror. Her hair was a mess, her lipstick was all worn off, and she looked tired. This was how
she looked the last time she saw Greg! She washed her face,
tidied her hair, then went down to catch a bus.

The after-work rush was beginning. There was already a
lineup at the bus stop. People jostled against her, and when
she finally got aboard she had to wait for a seat. While the
bus bumped along, with busy Toronto unreeling like a film
beyond the window, Jodie thought of the future, because
thoughts of the present would probably make her cry. She
couldn't possibly go on working for Greg. It was a good job,
but there were loads of great opportunities for computer
programmers.

The university, her alma mater, was doing interesting work in that field. They had got the contract to put the entire Oxford English Dictionary on disks. But that would be a job for data entry clerks by now. The interesting work on that project was already done. Her professor had tried to lure her onto his staff when she graduated. She was sure he could find a spot for her, and if not, there were plenty of businesses in the area.

So why did she feel as if her life was over? It was because she wouldn't be working with Greg, wouldn't even see him.... Of course she'd have to leave in the regular way, to avoid office gossip. And that meant two weeks' notice. Two weeks in the same building as Greg was unthinkable. Maybe she could make those two weeks her annual vacation. She had booked it for September, but in the circumstances, Greg would probably be delighted for her to switch the dates. Mr. Edison would be delighted. She'd have to remember not to call him Greg.

It seemed she had been sitting on the jiggly bus for half a lifetime, yet when she reached her stop, she was surprised to be there so soon. She got off near Lennie's Pizzeria. It was a garish-looking place with a blinking neon sign. Inside, red vinyl benches and white faux marble tabletops were further enlivened by Tiffany-style hanging lamps. The room wasn't full yet at four-thirty, which enabled her to find a seat with no trouble.

Hank was just coming from the kitchen with a steaming pizza on a footed stand when she entered. All the employees wore green jackets and funny little green and white caps. She found a table in Hank's section and waved at him. He came over right away.

"Hi, Jodie. You've taken a table for four. Mind moving to one of the smaller ones?"

"Sorry." He led her to a table for two in a corner. Her elbow hit the wall every time she moved. "Have you spoken to Bud this afternoon?" she asked.

"I heard all about it."

"Why did he go to the auditions?"

"I told him what you said about the pay scale. It seemed worth a try."

"I guess you guys will be staying in Toronto, huh?"

"That's for sure. Bud and his brother had a rare set-to. Greg met him in a subway station."

"Were you there? What did he say?" she asked eagerly.

"I wasn't there. Bud had planned to meet Gil and me here before he went on to work. That's when he told us about the meeting. It didn't quite come to blows, but there's not much hope for a reconciliation."

"That's too bad. Greg had agreed to Juilliard. I was still working on him about the summer job thing."

"He agreed to Juilliard?" Hank exclaimed. "Bud didn't say anything about that!"

"Then I guess Greg was too mad to tell him. Or maybe he changed his mind. He didn't even know Bud had applied. Isn't that incredible, the lack of communication? Nearly as bad as us," she added with a rueful smile. "You should have told me what you were planning, Hank."

"I know. I feel like a turkey, but for what it's worth, Gil and I plan to go back to school in the fall. I think that's why Bud really went to the Wonderland auditions. He felt bad about what you said, accusing him of leading us poor little lambs astray. He advised us to return and finish high school. He was hoping to meet up with some other musicians, to form another group. He's miles above Gil and me anyway—musically, I mean."

"Can I tell Mom and Mrs. Turner that you and Gil will be back?"

"Yeah. In fact, we'll tell them ourselves."

"Even better."

He looked shy and embarrassed. "There's no reason we can't call home. Or even go home, on a weekend or day off or something."

"We'd like that, and so would Duke."

Jodie ordered a pizza, and when Hank returned with it, he asked, "When are you leaving town?"

"My train goes at eight-thirty."

Hank sounded alarmed. "You mean tonight?"

"I've got a job, remember?"

"Since you're with your boss, that can't be a problem."

"That's what you think!"

"Is Greg leaving, too?"

"I imagine so," she said vaguely.

Hank drew a deep sigh of regret. "Well, that blows any chance of smoothing things out between Bud and his brother. I was hoping you could talk to them both, maybe arrange something about Juilliard...." He looked at her hopefully.

"I'm the last person he'd listen to."

"No way. He's really sorry he flared up at you. In fact, he wants to apologize."

A hopeful smile lit her eyes. "Did he say so?"

"He was downright penitent."

"What did he say?"

"He says he realizes you didn't set him up. It was just one of those things."

Bud! He was talking about Bud! "Oh, that's all right. We were all pretty upset and confused."

"So do you think you could talk to Greg?"

The manager had been casting sharp looks toward Jodie's table. "You'd better get to work before you get sacked. We'll talk later."

Even if the pizza had been good, which it wasn't, Jodie wouldn't have noticed. She was brooding on Hank's sugestion. Every fiber of her body objected to seeing Greg gain, especially in the role of supplicant. Let Bud do his wn smoothing out. The only problem was, he probably vouldn't do it. He was at that difficult age when proving his nanhood was of paramount importance. He had just staked is claim to maturity; it was asking a bit much for him to go rawling back to Greg. Yet his whole future hung on a neeting to reconcile the brothers.

Dammit! Greg was the one who should make the first verture. He was supposed to be the mature one, the great nanaging consultant. He could whip whole corporations nto shape, but he couldn't manage one young brother. A fit f anger seized her. She put down her fork and marched to he pay phone.

Thank heaven Greg hadn't left yet! she thought. He anwered on the second buzz. "Mr. Edison, it's Miss James ere," she said crisply. "I'd like a word with you before you eave town."

"I was just about to check out."

"Sorry to inconvenience you, but this is important. I can e there in fifteen minutes."

"Very well. I'll wait—for fifteen minutes."

"Wait until I get there," she said boldly, and hung up efore he could retaliate.

Jodie went back to her table, threw a bill on it to pay for ne pizza and spoke to Hank before leaving. "I've got to go. 'll phone you before I leave town. Bye."

She ran out of the restaurant and looked at the roads, logged with traffic and not a free taxi in sight. Her blood :arted to simmer. He'd wait fifteen minutes, while she left er dinner on her plate and tried to get a taxi at rush hour ɔ save his bacon! She had a few things she wanted to get off er mind before that meeting was over. And he had better ait!

Chapter Nine

Greg was waiting in the lobby of the hotel with his expensive leather luggage at his feet when Jodie hurried in. He was back in his role of Mr. Edison, wearing a lightweight business suit, shirt and tie. He had obviously showered, shaved and combed his hair. His impeccable grooming made Jodie acutely aware of her own disheveled appearance, and the reason for the difference. While she had been trying to help, he had been looking after *numero uno*, himself. She could have borne the injustice if he had smiled, or seemed a little happy to see her, or at least called her Jodie.

Instead, he gave her one short, impatient glance, looked at his watch and said, "What is it that can't wait until morning, Miss James?"

She adjusted her slipping shoulder bag, to keep her hands busy. "Only a matter of life and death, Mr. Edison. Sorry to trouble you."

It took all Greg's self-control to maintain the calm facade, when a volcano was raging inside him. He experienced a gamut of emotions: anger, sorrow and guilt; he hardly knew what he was doing. Jodie's words caused a painful lurch in his chest. He felt as if his heart had stopped beating. In a flash he saw a dreadful image of Bud, killed in a traffic accident, or worse—dead by his own hand. His eyes widened and the blood drained from his face. "Good God! Not Bud!"

"Don't get your hopes up. He isn't dead."

His erratic heart resumed its beat. "Has he been hurt?" he asked, still frightened.

"Yes, he has been very badly hurt, *by you*!"

He wanted to retaliate for that trick, but relief robbed him of vengeance and he soon had control of his temper. "You're talking about his sensitivities. I didn't realize he had any."

"He's different from his brother in that respect. Where can we talk?"

Again he glanced at his watch. "Will this take long?"

"It better not. My train leaves at eight-thirty." Without waiting for him to suggest a location, Jodie strode to the center of the lobby, where plush sofas were arranged in squares around a grandiose gilt coffee table. It wasn't the ideal arrangement for privacy, as some of the sofas were occupied. Personally, Jodie didn't care if the whole city heard her.

She dropped her purse on a sofa and sat down. Greg restrained his anger and impatience and sat beside her. "Well, what is this important matter?" he demanded.

She leveled a challenging look at him. "You didn't tell Bud he could go to Juilliard. Why not?"

"He didn't see fit to tell me he wanted to go."

She blew this poor pretext for a reason away with one glance. "*I* told you he wanted to go. You *knew* it. What did you want him to do, beg?"

"I can't prevent him from going to Juilliard—if he can afford it."

"Your excuse for working so hard all these years was to help Bud. Since you neglected his emotional welfare to do it, I think you owe him his education. Sometimes I wonder if you even like him. Can't you see how important this is to him?"

Greg was shocked at the unfairness of her charge. "What's important to him is associating with ruffians, and playing rock and roll."

"My brother is not a ruffian!" she shot back, heart banging. "And the only reason any of them are here is because you're too pigheaded to listen to what Bud's been trying for years to tell you."

He gave a disparaging smile. "So he decided to send you to convince me."

"Bud doesn't know I'm here."

"Then why *are* you here? This is none of your concern."

His haughty attitude cut through any lingering veneer of politeness. When she answered, her voice was raised, heedless of the other hotel patrons, who were beginning to look at them. "Since Hank is involved, I'm making it my concern. Unlike the Edisons, we Jameses stick together. I'm here because I care what happens to Hank, and I happen to like Bud, too. You're giving him a raw deal, using your financial weight to ruin his life." An elderly couple tutted in shock at her disclosure, and shook their heads at Mr. Edison.

"My aim is to save him from himself."

"You're not doing much of a job of it, are you? So far you've driven him out of his home, into the arms of the rock and roll crowd you hate so much. If he does end up on skid row, you'll know where to lay the blame."

The elderly couple were shamelessly inclining their heads now, to catch his answer. Greg hated making a public display, but he tried to ignore them. "I didn't drive him out! He sneaked away behind my back."

"Now why do you suppose he did that, Mr. Edison? Is it possible he knew from past experience you wouldn't listen to him?"

"He never talked to me!"

"He tried. You only wanted to lecture to him." The wise gray heads nodded in agreement. "You never listened, and you're not listening to me now. You're just trying to rationalize what you know is wrong behavior. Bud didn't bother telling you about Juilliard, because he knew you'd veto the idea."

"He didn't tell me because he lacked the intestinal fortitude. He knew I'd—*veto the idea*." Damn her eyes, she was right. "I'd want to discuss it rationally," he said, despising the weak, insincere sound of the words.

"If that's French for 'try to talk him out of it,' I think you've just admitted you're prejudiced."

"I am not prejudiced," he asserted firmly. A little biased, maybe, but dammit, he was responsible for Bud.

"You're trying to live Bud's life for him. That's worse than prejudice. It's—" She was having difficulty finding the right way to phrase her thoughts. "It's emotional cannibalism," she said angrily. "Maybe Bud didn't act as wisely as he should. He's young. But at least he knew he had to escape from you, before you destroyed him with your old-fogy ideas. You're older. You're supposed to be the mature, wise one. You save all your wisdom for work. Is that what really matters for you?"

Greg no longer noticed the older couple shaking their heads in chagrin at the folly of youth. In Jodie's speech, he was hearing echoes of Bud's charge: "You wouldn't understand. It doesn't have anything to do with money." It had sounded unreasonable and unfair when Bud said it, and it sounded unfair now. "That's ridiculous," he scoffed, but

he felt guilty. Maybe he'd paid just a little too much attention to business, and not quite enough to Bud. The adoles-
cent years were unsettling. He should have been closer to
Bud, to guide him. At such a young age it was hard to
choose a path for the rest of your life. They could have
worked out some compromise.

Jodie saw the uncertainty in his expression. She rushed on
to gain her point. "If you care about him, then give him
your blessing, tell Bud he can go to Juilliard. You owe it to
him."

"And he owes a little respect to me."

"He can't respect you if he doesn't respect himself." Greg
gave a startled look. She looked back with more sorrow than
anger now. "You're treating him like an object, a pawn in
your life. And you're worried about your stupid pride at a
time like this!"

"You're quick to accuse, Jodie." The name came out
unnoticed in his anger. "What you say about Bud might be
true. I admit there's a kernel of truth in it. I did want Bud
to work with me. I've been overly absorbed in business, and
I'm out of touch with my brother. What's your excuse?"

"What do you mean?"

"It wasn't only Bud who deceived me. You knew where
he was all along. You were helping him. You lied to me."

"I wasn't helping him all along!" she retorted angrily. "I
only found the boys this morning. And the only reason I
didn't tell you was that I knew you'd go storming in immediately, laying down the law. I wanted to try to reason with
you first, to convince you to let Bud attend college—one of
his own choice."

"I think I had accepted that...."

"Yes," she said, embarrassed. "But Bud had other conditions. He wanted to stay in Toronto for the summer, too,
and I had to try to talk you around to accepting that."

His jaw stiffened in rebuke. "Bud's not the one who lays down the conditions. The decision, and the terms, are mine. I daresay you might have achieved even those unrealistic terms, but I can't say I approve of your method." The older couple gave a sharp look at Jodie. She was under suspicion now, too. "I'm capable of listening to reason, despite what you think. You didn't have to use—" He came to a conscious pause.

A flame of red flared on her cheeks. "I hadn't even spoken to Bud yet when we—"

A little gasp came from the elderly lady. She took her husband's hand and led him away. Neither Jodie nor Greg noticed. They were completely absorbed in their own argument. A new feeling of turmoil had crept into the discussion when it took this personal turn.

A memory of that scintillating interlude in Nickie's apartment washed over Jodie, weakening her resolve. The intransigent person beside her hardly seemed like the same sensitive, loving man who had kissed her the night before. Perhaps there were echoes of that fiery passion in his anger now. How had love degenerated to this awful anger? She wanted to stop the whole argument, but dammit, she was right! And if he was as hard-nosed and unreasonable as he seemed to be, no sane woman could live with him. She shook away the wisps of memory to hear what he was saying.

"You had already spoken to me about Juilliard. I think the idea was there, to wind the old fogy around your finger."

Jodie was beyond words. She put her purse over her shoulder and stood up. "I've said my piece. You know where to find Bud if you want to talk to him."

Greg rose, towering over her. His face was set in a mask of fury. His dark eyes burned into her accusingly. "Do you deny it?"

She tossed her head. "What's the point? We all know you don't listen to reason. You'll believe what you want to. And since that's what you believe of me, I obviously can't go on working for you. I'll save you the bother of firing me. I quit."

This curt speech gave him a jolt. He felt a staggering sense of loss, but of course concealed it. "I have no excuse to fire you. You're a competent employee."

"I'm more than competent. I'm damned good at my job. And this wasn't a scheme to sue you for wrongful dismissal, Mr. Edison, if that's what you mean by *excuse*. My mind doesn't work that way. I just don't want to have to work for you any longer." She gave him a dismissing look and walked away. Even in blue jeans and a shirt, she looked impressive. Jodie walked away briskly, her head held at a proud angle that lent her dignity.

Greg felt a sense of panic. Things had gotten completely out of control. He'd never meant for this to happen. "Where are you going?" he called after her. He didn't follow her, and Jodie didn't stop to answer. He just watched, with a tearing inside, as she strode away. She was the best thing that had ever happened to him; now he was losing her. No, *losing* was the wrong word. She had never been his. She had just been using her charm to make him do what she wanted. The sensible thing was to let her go—but it didn't feel like the sensible thing at all. It felt as if the sun had fallen from the sky, leaving his world bleak and cold.

Jodie went to the desk and asked for her luggage. The clerk handed her her knapsack, and the shiny black box with the silver rose in the corner. It was eight o'clock. The dress box served as a reminder that if things hadn't turned out so badly she'd have been at the Mermaid Seafood House with Greg now, sharing an intimate table for two.

Since that was impossible, she took the stairs down to the underground passage to Union Station, then phoned Hank at work. "I spoke to Greg. I don't know what he's going to do about Bud, but I've done everything I can. You'll phone Mom, Hank?"

"Tomorrow for sure. I can't call her from work, and it'll be too late when I get home tonight. Tell her not to worry, eh, Jodie?"

"I will. Whatever happens, Hank, enjoy your summer. And I'll take good care of Duke."

"Thanks, Sis. I better go. The boss is giving me hard looks. Bye."

Jodie got her ticket, then took a seat on one of the benches scattered around the station. There was a quarter of an hour to wait for the train, if it was on time. She'd never thought she'd be going home alone. Tomorrow was Friday. She'd have to go in to work to give Greg—*Mr. Edison*—her written resignation. She'd write the letter and leave it with his secretary to avoid meeting him.

She wondered if he'd go to see Bud. He had admitted, grudgingly, that he was a little to blame. Of course, Bud was partly to blame, too. If he was going to decide to grow up and assert his rights, he should have done it before he left home. He shouldn't have sneaked off behind his brother's back, leaving Greg to wonder what might have happened to him.

As long as Hank and Gil were going to go back to school in the fall, the whole affair was a tempest in a teapot for her family. It didn't do kids any harm to get away from home and learn how to look after themselves. They'd be more appreciative of their homes once they'd had to do their own laundry and feed themselves. And of course pay for everything.

Her eyes wandered from time to time to the doorway leading to the hotel. If Greg came after her, he'd come through that arch. He knew she was taking the train. If he were a gentleman, he'd offer her a lift. Maybe he had gone to talk to Bud. She'd gladly give up hope of seeing him if she could be sure of that.

A constant stream of people passed through, but not Greg. He had been all dressed up. Maybe he had asked someone else to have dinner with him. He must know lots of women in Toronto. He had clients there. Maybe he'd just got into his snazzy sports car and driven home. Written it all off as a bad experience—brother, employee, girlfriend . . .

How dared he suggest that she was using her feminine wiles to manipulate him! For a brief instant she was flattered that he thought this was possible, but for him to believe she would do it was awful. She yanked angrily at her shoulder bag and scowled at the black dress box. She'd paid too much for the dress, and she'd probably never wear it again. Yet she was glad she had had it for last night.

The quarter of an hour seemed endless. It was too long to sit and think in private, where she could vent neither her anger nor her sorrow. There was sorrow there, too. Greg had seemed so nice, so thoughtful and considerate. But he had a blind spot as big as a football field if he thought he'd been a good brother.

He hadn't been a very good boss, either, when it came to that. He was fair enough, but cold and impersonal. She was glad she was leaving Edison's. If it weren't for having to clear out her desk, she wouldn't go back at all. She'd just send him a letter resigning. Her eyes traveled to the doorway again. But when the conductor made the boarding announcement for the train, Greg still hadn't shown up, and she had to fight back the tears.

She got on and found a seat with a vacant seat adjoining, relieved to be alone. She was in no mood to have to discuss the weather, the traffic or the high prices of Toronto

Waterloo seemed small-town and peaceful after the hectic pace of Toronto. She caught a cab home and recounted to her mother the news of what had happened.

"He's returning for school in the fall for sure?"

Everything had to be repeated two or three times before her mother could believe it. "Yes, and he'll call you tomorrow."

"Oh, I am glad," her mother said on a sigh of relief. "I'll call Mrs. Turner right away. Of course Mr. Edison already knows."

"Yes," Jodie said, and didn't go into all the unsavory details of her dealings with Mr. Edison. She'd have to do it soon, since she'd need some explanation for leaving her job, but not tonight. She'd had all the battering she could take for one day. "I'm going up for a nice relaxing shower, Mom. I'll be down soon."

"When Hank calls tomorrow, I'll tell him to have Gil call his mother, too." Mrs. James was already hurrying to the phone.

In Toronto, Greg's first fit of temper had worn off. After his argument with Bud in the subway station, he had been ready to give up in disgust and go home. He had been appalled to think of his brother living in some cramped, ugly quarters, and waiting tables in a beer hall. It was fatally easy to blame it all on Bud. The boy obviously had no judgment, no common sense, if he'd settle for existing in squalor. He'd soon tire of it and come home, suitably repentant and happy to go to Harvard. Greg was prepared to let him stew in his misery for a few weeks, or months if necessary.

After his meeting with Jodie, he had to reassess everything. She had delivered a few unpalatable truths that would take some digesting. He no longer planned to go home without talking to Bud again—rationally this time. No shouting, no accusations. He'd have to remember to listen, as well as talk. Bud wasn't a little kid anymore. When had he grown into a strong-willed man? Some secret corner of Greg's heart admired Bud's courage. Since Bud worked till midnight, a great many hours lay ahead, ones he'd have to get through alone.

He lingered as long as he could over dinner. His mind drifted to what should have been: his night with Jodie. He ate at the hotel, not caring where he was, or what he ate. It was just some place to pass the time, and nurse his aching heart. He was better off without her. What did he want with a beautiful, fun-loving woman who made him laugh—even at himself? A woman with eyes a man could drown in, and a thousand-watt smile that warmed him all over. Why should he want to feel young and happy, when he could be an old fogy? How dared she call him that!

"More coffee, sir?" the waiter asked. "We have decaf, so it won't disturb your sleep."

He *was* an old fogy. The waiter hadn't worried about disturbing his sleep when he was with Jodie.

"I'll have regular coffee, thank you," he said angrily.

At ten the waiters became restless, so he left. As it seemed his brother was going to be a musician, Greg decided to stop at some night spots and check them out. The concierge at the hotel suggested a few of the better ones.

Greg was happy to see they weren't all as bad as Ruby's. The music was louder than he liked; the performers' outfits looked a little strange to him, but not entirely unattractive for show business people. Being with Jodie the past two days in parts of the city he'd always avoided before had taught him to accept alternative styles of dressing. The tousled hair and leather and feathers didn't change a person's character. But he wouldn't allow himself the luxury of thinking of those hours with Jodie. Now he had to concentrate on Bud, and patching up the mess he'd made of their relationship.

Bud recognized his brother's Jaguar when he came out of work at midnight. Looking at it warily at first, he decided he should speak to his guardian man to man. Greg opened the door and Bud got in.

"We have to talk," Greg said.

"It's midnight. I'm bushed."

"Good, then now's my time to get you, when you're too tired to fight."

A joke? Greg didn't joke. "Don't count on it."

They went to a diner and talked until two o'clock in the morning. They were both engaged in an animated conversation. Bud finally got his turn to explain his hopes and plans.

"It sounds reasonable," Greg said. "I hope you believe I wouldn't have had any objection to Juilliard, Bud. I don't really want to live your life for you. But is this summer in Toronto really necessary?"

"It wouldn't have been, but it is now. I've influenced the other guys to come here. I can't just walk out on them. We've hired our apartment and practice hall. We've signed contracts for school dances. You wouldn't want me to break a contract. You always say a man's word is his bond."

"How many contracts are you committed to?" Greg asked.

"Only two so far, but we have other groups interested."

"That's pretty hard on you—young men, working day and night."

"You did it when you were my age, Greg. Once we get enough gigs to pay room and board we can ease up on the restaurant jobs. SWAK's been working so hard for so long, that we want to perform. It's really fun, Greg. And it'll do us a lot of good to get the experience of performing for bigger audiences. We even have a chance at some university dances. We never played anything but private parties and high schools before."

"That's fine for you, Bud, but aren't you being a little selfish? What do Hank and Gil get out of this?"

"Are you kidding? They love it. It's every kid's dream to be a rock star. I guess the dream was to be a high school football hero when you were young, but you must remember the feeling.''

''Yes, I'm not quite that old.''

''Kind of a fantasy, is what I mean. Don't worry, I won't let the guys get into any trouble. I steer a tight ship. At home, they both live in households headed by women. They need to get out and see how guys live. I see it as a summer camp experience, learning to take care of themselves.''

Greg didn't scoff at this rationalization. He even suspected that there might be a kernel of truth in it. Boys on the threshold of becoming men did want to try their wings. Strange as it seemed, he even believed that Bud would look after them. ''When did you go and grow up on me?'' he asked ruefully. ''I'm counting on you to keep those guys out of trouble. Their families are, too. I know you won't let us down.''

Bud beamed. ''Don't worry. I had a pretty good role model when I was growing up. If there's one thing I learned from you, it was a sense of responsibility. It was hard for a kid to appreciate, but now that I'm older, I do appreciate all you did for me, Greg. Now if I'd only taken the time to teach you how to have some fun in life.'' Bud grinned, but Greg knew he wasn't entirely joking.

''It's never too late to learn.''

Bud gave him a laughing look. ''You've got yourself one heck of a teacher in Jodie. She's really a nice woman, Greg.''

Greg gave him a questioning look. ''There's nothing like that between us.''

''Ah, if I were ten years older! I thought you two looked pretty keen on each other when I saw you outside Massey Hall. I hope this SWAK business hasn't come between you. She's really a special person, Greg. I know people say that about everybody now, but it's true about Jodie. She was always interested in our music. She'd listen to our practices sometimes, and bring us soft drinks and stuff. When we got our first gig, she went to hear us."

"She certainly has admirable qualities, but she wasn't quite honest with me in this business," Greg said vaguely.

"That's because she cares—about her brother, and me, and probably even you. She was trying to work out a compromise that was best for us all. What did she have to gain by involving herself, and especially by helping me? You're her boss. If she were trying to help herself, she'd have sided with you, wouldn't she?"

"I guess she would," Greg admitted. "But I don't see much evidence of her caring for me."

Bud just shook his head. "I know I'm young, but I'd say she's helped you a lot. She managed to mend the breach between us for one thing. You seem—nice." Greg scowled. "Nicer, is what I mean. More thoughtful, you know. More like the kind of guy a woman could care for." Bud examined his brother closely. Greg just rubbed his jaw pensively.

"I've got to get some shut-eye," Bud said, yawning. "The guys'll be wondering what happened to me. You'll be going back to your hotel?"

"I checked out. I'm driving home."

"You're welcome to crash with us. On the floor—no, I'll take the floor. You can have my bed."

"Thanks, but I have a feeling I won't be doing much sleeping tonight. I'll drive on home. Take care of yourself, Bud. Are you all right for money?"

"We're doing this on our own. Drive carefully, Greg. I'll probably be home some weekends when we're not performing, if that's all right with you?"

"That'd be nice."

"I'm sorry for all the hassle. It was just—I had to do something, you know?"

"I know. You had to live your own life. I'm sorry, too. It was mostly my fault."

"We'll share the blame. I guess we're both stuck with being pigheaded Edisons."

They parted as friends, better friends than they'd been for years. Greg drove the sixty miles home alone. A feeling of contentment eased the pain of Bud's having grown up on him. He'd be leaving home for good in the fall. It would be lonesome without him. Bud had often been a headache, as teenagers were bound to be, but he was basically a good kid.

Greg turned on the radio for company. One day he might hear Bud's music on the air. He was glad Bud hadn't given up his dream. Maybe he should have kept at his art.... But it wasn't the same. He hadn't had that desperate, driving ambition, and maybe not the talent, either. Art was just an emotional outlet for him now. Was he using art to sublimate other longings? Of course he went out with women, but he had never found that special one until...

The image of Jodie slid easily into consciousness. He knew it had been lurking there all evening. When he thought of her, it wasn't prim Miss James in her glasses with her pinned-up hair that he saw. It was the free spirit, with her flowing tresses and her impetuous ideas, like auditioning for a rock band. Had that been the problem with his love life all along? Was there more of Bud in him than he realized? He never could warm up to those buttoned-down career women he usually associated with. But he had certainly warmed up to Jodie when she let her hair down.

He was thirty-one. Bud obviously thought he was an old man. And Jodie had as well; she'd called him an old fogy. She disliked him so much that she even planned to quit her job. She'd do it too, if he didn't stop her. So he had to come up with a plan to stop her—somehow. A pigheaded Edison couldn't just stand there and watch his life be wrecked. Bud, at eighteen, was wise enough to know it.

The question was, could he convince Jodie that she needed him as much as he needed her?

Chapter Ten

Jodie rose like a zombie the next morning, after a restless sleep. It was the day she'd resign. Should she go to work at the usual hour? Or since she was going to quit, could she stop in later, just give Mr. Edison's secretary her letter of resignation, pack up her belongings and leave? She opted for going at the regular time in hopes that Mr. Edison wouldn't be there.

If he had taken her advice last night and gone to see Bud, he might have stayed overnight in Toronto. In any case, he usually spent his mornings in his office taking care of his correspondence, so morning was the best time to go.

After a quick shower, she sorted through her closet to select her most businesslike dress. She chose a pale blue one, severely tailored with a notched collar and white piping down the buttoned front. It might almost have been a uniform. She twisted her hair into its customary chignon and put on her glasses. The dark rims lent her a studious air and made her look more mature. Her shoes had a medium heel,

dressy and even feminine, but without suggesting flirta-
tion.

Instead of the casual purse she'd taken to Toronto, Jodie
used a small clutch bag and carried her briefcase. Before
leaving, she checked herself out in the hall mirror. Well, if
she did happen to see Greg, he wouldn't be able to find
anything wrong in her appearance today. She scowled and
called goodbye to her mother, who was just coming downstairs.

In fifteen minutes, Jodie was driving into her parking spot
at Edison's. The company had its own building. The front
of the gray stone edifice was landscaped with yews and
spreading junipers. A bed of white, low-lying alyssum bor-
dered a bank of red geraniums. It was all neat and tidy and
unimaginative, to match the proprietor, she thought with a
grimace. Of course a managing firm wanted to project a
solid, secure image.

Jodie's co-workers welcomed her back, bombarding her
with queries about her absence. The rumor of Bud Edison's running off to Toronto with her brother had leaked
out. She saw no reason to deny it, but she didn't give any
details of what had happened, except to say yes, the boys
had been found.

"Mr. Edison will probably be in a fit of temper," one
woman said.

"He isn't in yet?" Jodie asked unconcernedly.

"No, it's not like him to be late."

The first thing Jodie did when she sat down was to load a
word processing program into her computer. She then began to write her letter of resignation. She hadn't thought it
would be so hard to make it polite, yet unemotional. Every
phrase she typed sounded either rude or groveling. In the
end, she settled for the regulation format: "I regret to in-
form you that for personal reasons, I will be leaving Edi-

son's,'' followed by a routine mention of her enjoyment of her job over the past year.

She sealed the envelope and marched straight off to Mrs. Coombs, before second thoughts weakened her resolve. Mrs. Coombs was a middle-aged woman of statuesque proportions. Her tall frame was well padded, but she carried her weight well, and wore stylish clothes.

"Mr. Edison isn't in yet," Mrs. Coombs said. "I haven't heard whether he's back in town."

"It's not urgent. You can just give this envelope to him when he arrives," Jodie said.

She returned to her desk and began clearing it out. Her leaving would cause a lot of commotion among her co-workers, and she tried to do it quietly. Her immediate superior, Mrs. Banks, interrupted her at the job, asking for the sample sheets of custom-designed application software she'd been creating for a customer. Mrs. Banks was a nervous, angular woman with ginger hair worn short, like a boy's.

"I'm supposed to present them for approval at the meeting at eleven. Are you nearly finished, Miss James?"

Jodie realized that it was unprofessional to leave work half-done. She really should finish that task. It wouldn't take much more than an hour to run a sample test through the spreadsheet software.

"I'll have them by eleven, Mrs. Banks."

It was hard to concentrate on the job, when she feared every minute that Mr. Edison would appear. She knew he had come in. Although she hadn't actually seen him, she had heard Mrs. Banks tell another manager that Mr. Edison had returned from Toronto, and the weekly meeting was on.

Had he read her letter? She shouldn't have told Mrs. Coombs it wasn't urgent. Maybe he hadn't even opened it yet. But Mrs. Coombs would have told him whom it was from. If he cared, he would have opened it first and asked her to come to his office.

Mrs. Coombs had indeed told him. Jodie's was the first letter Greg read, and when he finished, he laid it on the desk and sat for a long time, looking at it with a worried expression. She certainly hadn't wasted any time! She was here, just around the corner, three doors away, and she might as well be on the moon. He couldn't talk to her in front of other employees, and he suspected she'd resent being called to his office like a recalcitrant schoolgirl. In any case he couldn't force her to stay.

A troubling memory of his futile effort to force Bud came to trouble him. Jodie was right; he did try to play God, trying to make everyone bend to his will. But at least he had to try to convince her to stay. He'd speak to her during the coffee break at ten-thirty, when the other employees were in a group, talking.

At twenty-five after ten, Jodie was just returning to her desk after delivering the spreadsheets to Mrs. Banks. Her phone was ringing. She hurried to catch it, forgetful for a minute of Mr. Edison. His deep voice caught her off guard. "Miss James, I have your letter. Can I speak to you for a minute, please? It might be better if you come to my office—more private," he added, to soften the command.

"You mean now?" she asked.

"As soon as it's convenient."

"All right. I'll be there in a minute."

Her co-workers were beginning to leave their desks in a mad dash for the coffee wagon. Jodie took out her compact and put on fresh lipstick, patted a few stray hairs into place, then went to Mr. Edison's office. Mrs. Coombs had left her desk, but his door was open. She saw him through the open door, bending over some papers on his desk.

He looked every inch the successful businessman, surrounded by the symbols of his success. Thick carpets, original paintings on the walls, a massive oak desk with the accoutrements of business: phone with a dozen buttons, a card file and a personal computer on a side table. Its inconvenient position told her he didn't use it much. The desk itself was a massive oak affair, with two chairs placed in front of it. A row of windows behind him gave a view of the busy street beyond. One side of the room held a sofa and coffee table for more informal meetings.

Her mind was in a state of tumult as she tapped lightly on the door.

Mr. Edison looked up from his desk and gazed at her. It was difficult to recognize Jodie, hiding behind the dark-framed glasses and with her beautiful hair bound up. Her dress looked like a uniform. A scowl drew his brows together. "Come in," he said brusquely, motioning to the chair by his desk.

Offended by his tone, Jodie went stiffly to the chair and perched on the edge of it. "I would like to leave as soon as possible, Mr. Edison. I thought I could take my holidays during my two weeks' notice."

Alarm rose to panic. She planned to leave immediately— today! In his worst imaginings, he thought he had at least two weeks to win her over. He uttered the first excuse that popped into his head. "That doesn't give me much notice! I have to find someone else to replace you. I thought you'd be here to train your replacement."

All he cared about was his business. He didn't give a damn that she was leaving. "Mrs. Banks can train her—or him."

"She'll be busy with all the paperwork of the McMurchy merger. There's still plenty to do there, tying up the loose ends. You're leaving us at a bad time."

Jodie wanted to appear professional, but as he was being perfectly selfish, she didn't plan to go far out of her way. "I'll stay and work for the two weeks, if that would help."

"It's hard to find a good programmer. They're in short supply."

"You can't expect me to give you six months' notice!" she said angrily. "Two weeks is all that's required, Mr. Edison. I'll stay for the two weeks."

"The search may take more than two weeks. You can't just leave—"

Not a word of regret about her leaving. No compliment on the good job she'd done! He expected her to bend over backward to help him, and get nothing in return.

"If it's the salary, I could do something about that," he said. This tack often worked.

She looked at him indignantly. "There isn't enough money in the bank to convince me to stay here a day longer than necessary. It that's all, Mr. Edison, I'll leave now for my coffee break."

"Dammit, you're being inconsiderate about this."

"*I'm* being inconsiderate!"

The phone rang before Jodie could begin to enumerate Mr. Edison's faults. She was sorry at the time, but after she had returned to her desk and cooled down, she decided it was a good thing the phone had rung, and she had taken advantage of the interruption to leave. It would be uncomfortable enough working for her last two weeks, without adding to it by telling Mr. Edison exactly what she thought of him.

Her breaths were fast and shallow, and her hands were trembling. She was in no shape to join the other workers, and working at her terminal was impossible, so she rearranged her desk till she had settled down. Mr. Edison didn't call her back to his office as she thought he might. He didn't drop by her desk later in the day either. The possibility that he wanted to keep her around for some reason other than her programming ability was soon forgotten. He didn't seek her out, and taking great pains to avoid him, Jodie was determined not to see him any more that day.

When Jodie returned home for dinner, she learned that Hank had phoned his mother, as he'd promised. It was through her mother that Jodie learned Bud Edison would be attending Juilliard School of Music in the autumn, and the other boys, Hank and Gil, would be coming back to finish high school.

Jodie was thrilled for Bud. "Mr. Edison agreed to Juilliard?" she asked.

"Yes, so Hank says. They got together last night and had a good talk."

She wondered if her lecture to Greg had anything to do with it. If so, she didn't regret her interference, no matter how disastrous it had been for herself. But she resented Greg for withholding that very important piece of news. Her mother found it odd, too. "All the time you were driving home from Toronto with Mr. Edison, he didn't say a word about it?"

"I came on the train, Mom. He stayed a while longer."

"Why didn't you tell me?"

"I guess it slipped my mind."

"The boys have got three gigs in Toronto so far, and one at some suburban tennis club for a dance," Mrs. James continued. "Since they have the van, they could come home and play some of the local gigs, but I suppose they wouldn't make any money by the time they paid their traveling costs."

"They probably would. It's not that far," Jodie said absently. Her mind was on other things. So the great Gregory Edison had caved in. He had listened to her, she was sure of it. She felt a glow of triumph, which had soon turned to annoyance. It was incredibly selfish and egotistical of Mr. Edison not to have told her what had happened. And he should have apologized, too, since he had apparently conceded that she was right.

Other than the phone call from Hank, nothing unusual happened. Jodie had to confess to her mother that she'd quit her job, and invent an excuse for her action. She said she couldn't get along with her boss. Then she called her professor friend about a job at the university, but he was away on holidays. She knew employment in her field wouldn't be hard to find, and as the position she preferred was at the university, she didn't bother trying for any other.

No new employee had been found to take Jodie's place at Edison's. Mrs. Banks spent as much time as possible with her, familiarizing herself with the details of Jodie's job. It would be for Mrs. Banks to teach the replacement, when she, or he, was found.

A week passed quickly. Jodie began to notice small changes in Mr. Edison's appearance and behavior. She saw him passing her office once in a sport shirt without a tie. That wasn't so very strange, since it was summer, but Mr. Edison always wore a tie, even on those rare occasions when he removed his jackets.

She learned from Mrs. Banks that he had left early one afternoon to play golf. That was even more bizarre. "I thought it was written in stone somewhere that he played golf on Saturday morning at ten." Mrs. Banks laughed.

Jodie mentioned the shirtsleeves and lack of a tie the day before. "He's changed," Mrs. Banks said, gazing at the window. "For instance, he didn't get his hair cut on the weekend. It's getting a little longer at the back than he usually wears it. I mentioned it, and he said, 'Oh, it's summer. I won't worry about it at the moment, Marj.' He called me Marj. Imagine! Next he'll be asking me to call him Gregory."

"You've been with him for five years. It's about time he called you by your first name," Jodie said.

"If we were ever going to use first names, the time would have been about four years and six months ago. Why now?

Something happened when Bud ran away. I'm convinced of it. Would you know anything about it?'' the brightly curious eyes bored into her. Was the whole office gossiping about that possibility?

"I can't imagine," Jodie said evasively.

Twice she had gone to speak with Mrs. Banks in her office, when Mr. Edison was there. In front of Mrs. Banks, however, they both acted as if nothing unusual had ever happened between them. Most of his business was with Mrs. Banks, which left Jodie free to study him surreptitiously.

She noticed the black hair growing a little lower on his neck, as Mrs. Banks had mentioned. She remembered how it felt between her fingers, crisp yet smooth, like raw silk. When he rested his hands on the desk, Jodie remembered how those long, strong fingers had held hers closely, protectively. Her eyes continued up his muscled, tanned arms, to his shoulders, all of which filled his blue shirt to perfection. She allowed herself a peep at his face. His eyes were down, looking at some papers, and she noticed how his long eyelashes curled, luxuriously over his lids. But his jaw was rugged, and his lips . . .

He glanced up suddenly, catching her, following her gaze, which by now had rested on his lips, remembering. Feeling a rush of embarrassment, Jodie excused herself from the office. Mr. Edison didn't say anything. He just looked as she told Mrs. Banks she'd return later. But there was something in the way he looked. . . .

She was curious how he would act if they were ever alone. On the Monday of her last week, she found out. It didn't happen in Mrs. Banks's office, but in the personnel office. The manager's secretary asked Jodie to fill out some forms regarding her departure. While sitting at a small desk in the corner, tackling her forms, Jodie looked up to see Mr. Edison walk in.

"Alice, have you received any replies to that inquiry on the dental insurance—" He glanced at Jodie and stopped in mid sentence. Their eyes met and held. Alice, looking at them, thought they both looked frightened, or guilty. It was Jodie who turned away first, resuming work on her form. Mr. Edison seemed rather confused. "That inquiry—" he said.

"About the dental insurance," Alice prompted.

"Yes. Yes, the er—insurance company—"

"Mr. Brock is handling it. He's out at the moment, but I'll see if there's anything in his files."

She went into the Personnel Manager's office, and Jodie sat on, pretending she didn't notice she and Greg were alone. He waited a moment, but when Mr. Brock's phone rang and Alice answered it in his office, he strolled over to where Jodie sat. He stood a few feet away from her.

"So, you'll be leaving us, Miss James," he said, in that hearty way that didn't successfully mask his discomfort.

She glanced up briefly. "Yes, on Friday."

"Sure we can't talk you out of it? We haven't found anyone to replace you."

"Quite sure."

"Have you found another job?"

"I hope to work at the university. Professor Weber is on vacation at the moment, but I'm confident he'll find something for me."

"Why don't you stay on with us till September?" He came a step closer.

Jodie looked up and saw he was leaning toward her. He put a hand on the back of her chair, familiarly. She could almost feel some electric vibrations at his closeness. Her heart pounded, and she looked away from his dark eyes with the seductively curling lashes. "I'm not trying for a position on the teaching faculty, Mr. Edison. There are several research projects that continue year-round," she said, trying to keep her voice steady. But his nearness made it difficult.

"So you'll be leaving Friday." His voice was softer now. Was that stifled regret she heard?

"Yes."

"I hope you'll come to our annual picnic on Saturday. It's at Fairley Park, as usual."

"I won't be an employee by Saturday," she pointed out.

"Don't be ridiculous! That's splitting hairs," he said angrily. She looked up then, and saw the scowl that drew his brows together. His head had come a few inches closer. "You were an employee when the invitations were sent out. I hope you'll come, Jodie."

It was the "Jodie" that caught her off guard, and sent her heart thudding painfully in her chest. She watched as his scowl softened to hope. Had he used her name by accident? He had called Miss Martin Alice, too. Perhaps using first names was just a new office policy. There was nothing personal about that. But the way he said it, the way he was looking at her, was very personal. "Will you come?" he asked.

She had the impression he was holding his breath till she answered. "I'll be there if I'm free."

Alice Martin came out of her boss's office with the file and the moment was over. Mr. Edison gave Alice an impatient look. Jodie thought he was going to send her off on some errand, but he just took the folder and left.

"I don't know what's gotten into Mr. Edison," Alice said. "He never called me Alice before. I wonder if I should call him Gregory."

"I have no idea."

"Do you still call him Mr. Edison?" Again that brightly curious look was leveled at her.

"Yes," Jodie said, and continued her work. She didn't want to discuss Mr. Edison. She wanted to go home and cry.

She hardly ever cried, but lately she always felt on the edge of tears.

Jodie didn't see Mr. Edison on Tuesday, and on Wednesday and Thursday he was out of town. That left just one day, Friday, when she might see him, perhaps for the last time. She knew he was in the building, but he didn't come to her desk, or ask her to his office. Her co-workers were taking her out for a farewell lunch, and they all dressed up for the occasion. They were taking her to the lovely dining room at the Seagram Museum.

Mrs. Banks had told Jodie that she needn't come back to work after lunch. "There won't be much work done in any case, since we'll all be busy preparing for the company picnic tomorrow. Mrs. Coombs and I are going over to Fairley Park this afternoon to see that everything's ready."

Maybe Mr. Edison was waiting till the last minute to speak to her. Maybe he planned to stop by her desk as she was leaving that afternoon.... "I don't mind coming back," she said.

"There's really no point. Why don't you just pack up your things now and you can go on home after lunch? It's such an anticlimax, going back to work after the farewell party."

"Thanks, Mrs. Banks. That's very nice of you."

"Don't thank me. It was Mr. Edison's idea. You'll be coming to the picnic tomorrow?"

Greg had suggested it! Then he knew she wouldn't be back! And still he didn't come to say goodbye. "I—I haven't decided," Jodie said. "It's really a family day for the children."

"Oh, but the dinner dance in the evening is for the adults—you'll come to that!"

It was the highlight of the year. The Christmas party was a small affair in the office, with sherry and the distribution of the Christmas bonuses. The annual picnic was the big event, with a day outdoors for the family, and an adult bash in the evening.

If Greg came to say goodbye, she'd go to the party. "I'll go if I can," she said lamely, to leave her options open. Mr. Edison didn't come to say goodbye. At eleven-thirty she began packing up her belongings, and at noon the group left for lunch.

The lunch was lovely. Pink tablecloths, decorated with bouquets of flowers, added a festive touch. Her co-workers had chipped in and bought her a gold chain necklace, with a charm in the shape of a computer terminal, which Mrs. Banks presented. Jodie felt tears sting her eyes as she read the card, signed with all their names and good wishes. It was an emotional moment, and underlying it all was the knowledge that she had missed her chance for a private word with Greg. He hadn't bothered coming to say goodbye. Always the consummate professional, she managed a short, heartfelt speech, which received rousing applause.

They were just deciding on dessert when the waiter came to their table with a large bottle of champagne in a bucket. "Oh, girls! You shouldn't have!" Jodie laughed.

The group exchanged embarrassed glances. They hadn't! "Compliments of Mr. Edison," the waiter said, smiling, while he popped the cork with a flourish.

Jodie looked at him, hoping that he'd hand her a card, and feeling prematurely the embarrassment of opening it in front of everyone. But there was no card.

"Oho!" Mrs. Banks exclaimed. "So there *was* something between you and Mr. Edison in Toronto, eh Jodie? Now the truth comes out. He's never sent champagne to a going-away party before." They all laughed, taking it for a good joke.

"He's just glad to be rid of me." Jodie laughed along with them and then sipped the champagne. But while the others were impressed with Mr. Edison's thoughtfulness, she thought it was a cold way to say goodbye. She decided right then that she definitely wouldn't attend the office picnic, not if Mr. Edison sent her a special engraved invitation.

Finally the farewell luncheon was over and Jodie left, promising to keep in touch, and thanking her friends one last time. She supposed she'd have to thank Mr. Edison for the champagne, too. She'd write him a note, because if he couldn't be bothered to drop by her desk, she'd be damned if she'd lift the phone and talk to him.

Chapter Eleven

Jodie stopped at a travel agent's on her way home. She had planned her annual vacation for the first two weeks of September, and had reservations for a flight to the West Coast at that time. She'd have to cancel that trip. She was on enforced holidays now, and couldn't take another two weeks in September. The travel agent tried not to laugh in her face when she asked to reschedule. There wasn't a single seat available until November, unless she wanted to stand by for a possible cancellation. Jodie couldn't see spending her holidays hanging around an airport in Toronto on the off chance of getting a seat.

She got a refund and drove to the railway station. A train trip out west might be fun. It would give her a chance to really see her country. The prairies, the timberlands around the lakehead, the Rocky Mountains, the Pacific coast. The reservations clerk at the railway office was more polite. He didn't laugh at her, but the story was the same. No vacancies until the fall.

The other possibility, unless she wanted to drive herself, was the bus. Jodie refused to even consider a three-thousand-mile bus trip across the continent, not to mention the return trip. She went home and told her mother, first about the going-away party, then about her ruined holidays.

"What a pity about your trip! I never could understand why you quit your job so suddenly," her mother said, still perplexed after two weeks.

"I just wasn't getting along with my boss, Mom," Jodie said vaguely.

"Couldn't you have spoken to Mr. Edison? He might have transferred you to some other department. He seemed very nice when he was here."

Jodie didn't correct the misunderstanding about which boss she'd been referring to. It was an injustice to Mrs. Banks, but her mother didn't know Mrs. Banks, so it seemed a harmless injustice.

"There's only one computer department, so I couldn't be transferred," Jodie explained. "I'd rather work at the university anyway. As soon as Professor Weber gets back, I'll get a job. Don't worry."

"But meanwhile your vacation's ruined. You should go away to a cottage at least, where you can swim and do some boating. Why don't you call some of your friends?"

Jodie was eager to get away somewhere, anywhere, for a while. She just wanted to get out of the town where Gregory Edison lived. She felt if she could put at least a few hundred miles between them, she could think straight. "I think I'll drive to Quebec City," she said, after pondering a moment. There had been a poster at the travel agent's office describing it as a little corner of France in North America. It showed a narrow, crooked, cobblestoned street that looked like France. It would be different. She'd get a chance to explore some of the historical spots of her country, and practice her French. "Why don't you come with me, Mom? We could leave tomorrow."

"I couldn't do that, dear. Hank's coming home tomorrow."

"You didn't tell me that!"

"You were so full of news, I forgot all about it. He'll just be home for an overnight stay. He has an engagement in town tomorrow night."

"Where's he playing?"

"I'm not quite sure. One of the clubs, he said."

"Well, in that case I suppose I'll stay until he leaves. I'd love to hear how he's getting along in Toronto. About Quebec—are you interested?"

Her mother's reluctance was obvious. "Only if you can't find anyone else to go with. You know I don't much care for traveling."

"You don't have to come if you have no desire to. Of course I can find someone to go with." But on such short notice, it wouldn't be easy.

On Friday evening, Jodie made a few desultory phone calls to friends and former classmates. She hadn't consciously realized before how many of them had got married, or engaged, or left the city for greener pastures. She felt as if she had been left behind in the onward rush of life.

Hank arrived home early Saturday afternoon. He came bounding in, full of youthful vigor and tales of his adventure. It was hard to tell who was happier, Hank or Duke. For an hour Hank regaled them with his experiences in the big city, while Duke curled jealously at his feet, insisting on attention. The summer away from home was good for Hank. he seemed a little more mature already.

"Where are you playing tonight?" Jodie asked. A deep feeling of dissatisfaction had been growing in her since Friday afternoon, when her trip out west fell through. It was partly boredom, but she sensed that it was more than that. Her whole body felt strained and tense, as if in anticipation of—something. Every time the phone rang, she jumped a foot.

At last she admitted that what she was waiting for was Greg to call, and since he apparently didn't intend to to that, she needed a diversion. She decided that if the gig was at some public place, she would stop by to watch SWAK perform. At least it would be something different.

"A company party. Bud set it up—seven hundred and fifty bucks, and they supply the sound system."

A company party—well, that surprised her.

"Where is it being held?" Mrs. James asked.

"At Fairley Park."

Jodie stiffened in surprise. "The Edison party?" she demanded.

Hank grinned. "The Edison party! So that's it! I wondered how Bud's brother got us such a great gig. But if it's Edison's own party, you'll be there, Jodie!" He smiled in pleasure.

"She quit her job," Mrs. James announced, in a voice of doom. They had to discuss that for a while.

"They'd still let you go to the party, wouldn't they?" Hank said. "I mean especially since SWAK's playing, and you and Greg..."

Jodie spoke up quickly. "Yes, I can go to the party if I want to. Maybe I will."

It would be silly not to go. She couldn't think of one single excuse to give Hank for not going. It was making too much of her brief entanglement with Greg to avoid the party because he'd be there. Greg might get the idea she was staying away because of him, and she didn't want him to think he influenced her behavior, one way or the other.

She wouldn't go to the afternoon picnic, though. It was really for the employees' children. In fact, she wouldn't attend the dinner either. She was only going to hear Hank and the boys play, and she wouldn't go until it was time for them to play. That would show Mr. Edison exactly why she was there, in case he had any doubts.

Of course that was no reason she shouldn't look her best. At the back of her mind rested the image of a mint-green dress. But no, she wouldn't wear that. That was too redolent of memories. She chose to wear a fancy sundress instead. This one was royal blue, with a full skirt edged in eyelet embroidery. The top hugged her body like a glove, and nipped in to her small waist. She pulled her hair up into loose rivulets of curls, from which a few tendrils escaped, creating a romantic impression. At her ears she hung earrings arranged in a dangling cascade of pearls.

Before leaving the house, she spun around in front of her mirror, satisfied with the way she looked. The image she admired was a sophisticated woman, an elegant woman unlike Miss James, with her glasses and tailored suits. The full skirt billowed when she walked, the edge of eyelet suggesting a flirtatious petticoat.

Her mother was visiting with Mrs. Turner when she came down. Both woman complimented her on her outfit, then her mother said, "Who are you going with, Jodie?"

"I'm going alone," Jodie said. For the first time, it occurred to her that she should have invited someone to escort her. All the women at work had been talking about their dates. There were single men at work, but they'd probably all be attached. How could she have forgotten to ask a date!

"Jodie just decided at the last minute to go to hear the boys play," her mother explained to Mrs. Turner.

"I'm sure Jodie has no lack of boyfriends." Mrs. Turner smiled.

Of course! She was just going to hear SWAK play. She didn't need a date to just listen. But she regretted that she hadn't asked someone to go with her, in case Mr. Edison got the idea she hoped to dance with him. Was that why she hadn't asked anyone? Did some stupid, secret corner of her heart think he'd want to spend the evening with her, and bring her home? He had probably invited a girlfriend. He'd think she couldn't scrape up a date for even one night.

She hurried out of the house before her mother could take notice of her strange mood. The mood deepened as she drove out toward Fairley Park. She must be crazy, getting all dressed up and going alone to a dance. She'd look ridiculous! She couldn't go. That was all. And she couldn't go home this early either, to face her mother and Mrs. Turner.

In a fit of indecision and confusion, she turned around and drove to Victoria Park. Turning off the ignition, she just sat in the car, watching the ducks and geese take their final waddle to the pond before settling in for the night. When she realized where she was, and what she was doing, she couldn't believe her own foolishness. She was acting like a teenager with her first crush. And what was worse, she felt like one. Her mind seemed to be burning up with imaginings and regrets. She had never had a crush of such huge dimensions on anyone, not even when she was a schoolgirl.

It went beyond a crush. You certainly couldn't have dropped out of high school because of a crush, but she had quit her job. Gone strutting off in a huff, like a kid. Greg must have thought she was ridiculous. Even when he asked her to reconsider, she kept sulking, nursing her grievances. She had won the battle: Bud was going to Juilliard, and the boys were staying in Toronto for the summer, so why was she still angry with him? Maybe he hadn't told her about his brother because he thought she already knew. He might think Bud had told her. But there was still the issue of her little deception. She couldn't blame him if he never forgave her.

It wasn't his fault if he didn't love her. If anyone should have been sulking, it was Greg, but he was behaving in a perfectly civilized way. He had sent champagne to her farewell luncheon. She should have called that afternoon to thank him.

The evenings were long in early July. The sky was still flushed with a pearly pink at the western horizon at nine-fifteen, when Jodie gave herself a mental slap. She was a mature woman after all, and it was time she started acting like one.

She would go to the dance, and if she met Greg, she'd be polite and adult. She'd thank him for the champagne. She'd just stay to hear SWAK play one or two numbers, then leave. She wanted to hear the boys play professionally, as she'd only heard them perform once in public, at a high school dance two years ago when they were just beginning. Now they'd acquired some snazzy costumes and more high-tech equipment. She put her car in gear, then drove toward the highway. As the sun set, she drove into the swiftly approaching darkness, which was relieved by the lights of many roadside signs of motels and other businesses.

The Fairley Park complex was partially obscured by trees, but she knew it consisted of various athletic facilities, as well as a huge banquet hall and dance floor. She parked her car, then went into the building. The dance was supposed to begin at nine. When she arrived at nine-thirty, it was well under way. From the dance hall came the rhythmic beat of Gil's drums, luring her on.

Slipping into the darkened room, she stood looking and listening. Her first thought was of Greg. It was hardly a thought really, more of an instinctive action to look for him. She was half relieved and half disappointed when he was not to be seen among the crowd. With a last glance all around, she turned her attention to the stage.

It felt strange, to see Hank dressed in a black shirt, dripping with scarves, all glittering, shining like jewels. He must have been wearing a half dozen of them. Bud was wearing something similar, and both of them were playing their hearts out, while moving around the stage, posturing with their instruments. Multicolored lights throbbed, lending a surreal quality to the performance. The band had improved since the last time she'd heard them. They played with sure precision now.

Entranced by the picture, she didn't pay much attention to the music at first, except for the throbbing insistence of the drums. They couldn't be ignored. But when Bud came forward to take his guitar solo, she came to attention. It was a ravishing, haunting melody, and Bud played it with sensitivity and expression. His face was enraptured, feeling the music as if he were drawing life from it. It was all there to see on his face. It was strange to consider that Bud Edison had conceived this music, arranged it and was now playing it in public.

She stood, listening and thinking, no longer conscious of being alone, or feeling strange. She watched Hank and Gil, too. They were in their element. Through Bud's music, two shy boys had been transformed. They wouldn't be shy loners when they went back to school. But the real victory was Bud's. He had managed the whole miracle, and despite all the resultant trouble, she wasn't sorry she'd helped make it possible for him to go on with his dream. If he could do this well with a couple of untrained kids, what would he be capable of once he was fully trained, and working with professional musicians?

Some of the people just stood around the edge of the room, listening, others were dancing. Jodie began to sway instinctively to the music.

Across the room, Greg had seen her enter, and for him the night began. He stood still, just breathing great gulps of relief and pleasure. He marveled at how beautiful she looked, like a sea nymph, so lithe and graceful, with a waist he could span with his two hands. Her hair suited her now, so soft . . . inviting. He wanted to feel its satiny smoothness.

It had been a long, hot, busy, confusing day. As the host of the picnic, he had to be on hand, organizing races, distributing prizes, cooking hot dogs and making ice cream cones. He hadn't really expected Jodie to come to the picnic. He had hoped she'd be at the cocktail party that preceded dinner. That would have given him a chance to speak to her.

When she didn't show up at the cocktail party, he'd shifted his hopes forward to dinner. His company wasn't so large that he was unable to check out every table. Before the soup was finished, he assumed she wasn't coming at all. It had been nearly impossible to sit making polite conversation while his mind was full of Jodie. By the time dinner was halfway through, however, his hopes had reemerged. She wouldn't miss this chance to hear SWAK play. That was why he'd hired them. She'd come for the dance—probably with a boyfriend, which would complicate matters, but she'd come.

He was in the dance hall at nine sharp, and had been watching the doorway ever since. When she entered, every muscle in his body tensed, and when he saw she was alone, he felt a wave of relief engulf him. After he caught sight of her, he allowed himself a moment to listen to Bud's music, and appreciate it. It seemed incredible to him that little Bud had created this music, and this show.

When Jodie began to sway to the music, Greg was afraid someone would ask her to dance before he got to her. He quickly began skirting the edge of the room toward her. Greg walked softly up behind her. He put one arm lightly around her waist and said, "Dance?"

Startled, Jodie turned to find herself staring into Greg's navy-blue eyes. His head was only inches from hers. Most important of all, he was smiling that familiar, intimate smile that said so much. At times she thought she must have imagined that look. It had vanished without a trace after their argument. She didn't say anything, but an answering smile grew slowly on her lips, and spread to light her eyes. His arm tightened around her waist as they moved to the dance floor.

Jodie was surprised at how well he danced, especially to modern music. She had obviously misread her boss. This wasn't the first time he'd gone dancing. In the heat of a summer's night, he had taken off his jacket and wore a casual, open-necked shirt. With his hair grown a little longer, he seemed a different person from the man she'd known days before as Mr. Edison. Talking was impossible on the dance floor, with the music blaring, so she just gave herself over to the rhythm, and moved with it. Their bodies didn't touch, but he seemed to be drawing her close with his unrelenting gaze.

When the music stopped, there was a loud round of applause. Jodie and Greg clapped louder than anyone else. "Not bad for kids," he said. She could see he was bursting with pride. It glowed from his smiling face.

"And you wanted to make him into a bean counter," she reminded him.

He enfolded her hand in his and pulled her closer to his side. "Are you going to say 'I told you so,' Miss James?"

"Certainly not, Mr. Edison, since you already know it."

They walked from the crowded dance floor into the hall, where guests were milling around the bar, farther along. "I was afraid you weren't going to come," he said.

"I wanted to see the boys perform."

He stopped and quirked an eyebrow at her. "I hoped that might lure you here," he said.

"Is that why—" She bit the words back, before she made a fool of herself. As if he had arranged all this just for her!

"That, and to satisfy my own curiosity. I'd never heard Bud's band play before. Of course I figured SWAK could probably use the money, too. It's hard on the kids, working in those sweat shops, trying to meet their obligations, playing their music in those clubs until the wee hours. The inspiration of asking them was to make sure you'd come. The other advantages occurred to me later."

Jodie felt a golden warmth seep through her body, as if the sun were shining inside her. "It worked. Here I am."

His fingers tightened on hers. "Here we are," he said. "We have to talk, Jodie. Let's go somewhere."

"You can't leave your own party!" she exclaimed, shocked that the idea had come from the very proper Mr. Edison.

"We'll come back later. I want to hear more of that music."

"What did you have in mind?"

His eyes focused on her lips, and he said in a husky voice, "What do you think?"

She swallowed a lump in her throat and said, "Oh," in a small voice.

"Exactly," he murmured, while his eyes ravished her.

He led her out into the warm darkness of the night. The touch of his hand on her arm sent prickles along her skin. Tables and benches were scattered amid the trees, where the picnic had been held that afternoon. The place was abandoned and quiet now, except for the muted sounds of summer. There was a gentle rustle of branches swaying, and a cicada's intermittent chirp. A full, luminous moon hung low in the sky, like a white balloon floating in the black void of space.

He stopped at one of the tables and leaned against it, facing her. They stood close together. "I was afraid you weren't going to come," he repeated.

"I wasn't going to. You seemed so glad to get rid of me, celebrating it with champagne," she said with a teasing look. "For which I never thanked you, incidentally. Thanks, boss."

His fingers tightened painfully on hers, and when he spoke, she heard the pent-up passion. He had felt the same frustration that she had. "I didn't want you to go! But how could I prevent it? I tried everything I could think of. More money, guilt."

What a pair of fools they had been. "You didn't try telling me you wanted me to stay," she pointed out.

Greg's brows drew together in confusion. "Wasn't that taken for granted? Why else was I trying to entice you to?"

"Programmers are in short supply," she reminded him. "That's what you said."

Greg gave a gesture of disgust for his own folly. "I'm an idiot. How could I tell you I loved you, when you'd just called me an old fogy, and praised Bud for trying to escape from me? You made me sound like a—a destroyer."

Love! The word came at her like a rifle shot. She couldn't speak for a minute. When she did, her voice was breathless. "You said worse things to me. You accused me of—"

His hands moved possessively up her arms, pulling her insensibly closer. "Don't even remind me. People say stupid things when they're upset, and feeling guilty. You were

right. I didn't listen to Bud—or you. I'm listening now, if
you have anything to say.'' His eyes glittered darkly in the
moonlight as he gazed at her.

She felt suddenly shy. "I think you did the right thing,
and I'm happy—for Bud and you. It wouldn't have worked
out, trying to make a businessman of him.''

"He's his own man, as he should be. You did the right
thing, too, to give me that much-needed lecture. Since you
thought I was some kind of monster, it took guts.''

"I'm not afraid of monsters." She smiled. His arm went
around her waist, and pulled her close against him in a
jerky, impatient movement. The heat of his body and the
firm masculine fiber and sinew of it excited her. It felt so
safe, so right.

"Do you think you could learn to love one?" he asked.

She stifled an exultant sigh of relief. "Nope. I never could
have loved you the way you were. I guess that's why I had
to change you.

His smile stretched to a grin. He cocked his head and just
looked at her a moment, then lowered his head. His lips
nibbled her ear, sending a trail of hot steam along her veins.
"I guess it's safe to change now. Since some of my
employees are younger than I am, I don't have to stand on
my dignity. I used formality as a crutch, because I was unsure of myself. You're the one responsible for the change.
I'm putty in your hands. Change away,'' he murmured.

"I think I've got you about right now. Not too stiff,
but—'' His lips moved across her face with a gentle rough-
ness, to find her lips, and then he muffled them with a kiss.

A shattering explosion occurred inside her. It seemed the
sky had split and released a shower of stars and moon-
beams. His arms tightened and he crushed her against him,

there in the moonlight. Her body mated with his, her soft-
ness melting to match his masculine contours.

His lips firmed, and her concentration focused on the
magic of that kiss. It was consuming fire and passion, softened to tenderness by love. Even in his ardor he was gentle,
until she encouraged him. His hand moved over her naked
back, sending an involuntary shudder of longing through
her. She placed a hand on his cheek, to stake her claim.
Then his kiss became roughly demanding.

When her lungs felt as if they might burst, Jodie relaxed
her hold and Greg lifted his head. He looked at her with a
wildly distracted look. "Does that mean you forgive me?"
he asked, in a husky voice.

She smiled, not trusting herself to speak. For some
inexplicable reason, she wanted to cry again. It was the pure
bliss of the moment that caused the sensation. "Did I thank
you for the champagne?" she said, quite irrelevantly.

Greg didn't find it irrelevant. "Yes, you did. I'm glad you
liked it. Will you come back to work?"

"I don't know. It doesn't really matter, does it?"

"No, it doesn't matter. I got Bud back by letting him go.
It's not really a programmer I want. It's you—whatever
makes you happy. As long as you love me..."

"I do love you, Greg."

He closed his eyes and leaned forward, his forehead
touching hers. "Amen," he said.

The wail of a guitar rent the air. "You've got to hear this
one. It's SWAK," Jodie said.

"Who else?"

"No, I mean the song is SWAK."

"Silly name. What does it mean anyway?"

"Greg," she said with a laugh, "didn't you ever write to
your high school sweetheart? It means sealed with a kiss."

"I never had a girl in high school. You're my first sweetheart. Shouldn't we seal it with a kiss?" He smiled, and pulled her into his arms.

*   *   *   *   *

COMING NEXT MONTH

#712 HARVEY'S MISSING—Peggy Webb
A Diamond Jubilee Title!
Janet Hall was in search of her missing weekend dog, Harvey, but
what she found was Dan Albany, who claimed Harvey was *his*
week*day* dog. Would the two ever agree on anything?

#713 JUST YOU AND ME—Rena McKay
The Loch Ness monster was less elusive than the blue-eyed
MacNorris men of Norbrae Castle. Vacationing Lynn Marquet
was falling fast for Mike MacNorris, one of the mystifying
Scottish clansmen . . . or was she?

#714 MONTANA HEAT—Dorsey Kelley
Nanny Tracy Wilborough expected to find peace of mind in
Montana. What she hadn't counted on was exciting rodeo
performer Nick Roberts lassoing her heart!

#715 A WOMAN'S TOUCH—Brenda Trent
When Troy Mayhan first met neighbor Shelly Hall, they literally
fell into each other's arms. Now the sexy ex-football player was
determined to have her fall again—in love with him!

#716 JUST NEIGHBORS—Marcine Smith
Loner Wyatt Neville had never had a sweet tooth—or been
tempted to indulge in romance—until delectable Angela Cowan
moved her cookie factory next door to his home. . . .

#717 HIS BRIDE TO BE—Lisa Jackson
The contract said she was his bride to be for two weeks only. But
two weeks was all it took for Hale Donovan to know that Valerie
Pryce was his love for a lifetime.

AVAILABLE THIS MONTH:

A celebration of motherhood by three of your favorite authors!

JENNIFER GREENE
KAREN KEAST
EMILIE RICHARDS

This May, expect something wonderful from Silhouette Books — BIRDS, BEES AND BABIES — a collection of three heartwarming stories bundled into one very special book.

It's a lullaby of love . . . dedicated to the romance of motherhood.

Look for BIRDS, BEES AND BABIES in May at your favorite retail outlet.

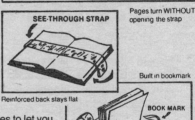

Silhouette Special Edition

proudly presents

Taming Natasha
by
NORA ROBERTS

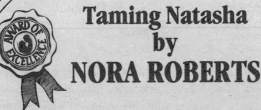

Once again, award-winning author Nora Roberts weaves her special brand of magic this month in TAMING NATASHA (SSE #583). Toy shop owner Natasha Stanislaski is a pussycat with Spence Kimball's little girl, but to Spence himself she's as ornery as a caged tiger. Will some cautious loving sheath her claws and free her heart from captivity?

TAMING NATASHA, by Nora Roberts, has been selected to receive a special laurel—the Award of Excellence. This month look for the distinctive emblem on the cover. It lets you know there's something truly special inside.

Available now

TAME-1A

AVAILABLE NOW—

the books you've been waiting for by one of
America's top romance authors!

DIANA PALMER

DUETS

Ten years ago Diana Palmer published her very first
romances. Powerful and dramatic, these gripping tales
of love are everything you have come to expect from
Diana Palmer.

This month some of these titles are available again in
DIANA PALMER DUETS—a special three-book collection. Each book has two wonderful stories plus an introduction by the author. You won't want to miss them!

Book 1
SWEET ENEMY
LOVE ON TRIAL

Book 2
STORM OVER THE LAKE
TO LOVE AND CHERISH

Book 3
IF WINTER COMES
NOW AND FOREVER

Available now at your favorite retail outlet.

 *Silhouette Books*®

DP-1A